## "Can't remember or can't think straight?" a male voice asked from behind her.

Ali froze. She knew that voice. It had whispered deliciously naughty intentions into her ear not so very long ago.

Her eyes moved along the ground from where she knelt with Chris, her breath caught tight in her chest. Blood began to thunder between her ears as a pair of leather shoes came into view and walked to the opposite side of Chris. It was all she could do not to cry out as the owner of the shoes came into view as he kneeled across from her. *Oh, she knew him, all right.* She knew him intimately. And she didn't know him at all.

As their eyes met Ali physically felt the breath being sucked out of her body.

*The Suit.*

Images flickered past her mind's eye of their bodies tangled together in a series of sexual acrobatics she'd never believed possible. A wash of pleasure rippled through her and it was all she could do to keep her jaw clamped firmly shut.

She'd never asked him his real name. Nor had he of her. That had been their deal. One night only.

Dear Reader,

This book was a real crackerjack for me, and an absolute hoot to write. A book full of muscly rugby players and a dreamboat of a team doc? Woo-hoo!

I am a *big* rugby fan—not that I know any of the teams or players or rules... I just love the dedication and commitment the players show to the game—and they're respectful to boot. Just like the perfect hero.

Ali is a great heroine—I really, *really* like her a lot. Mostly because she was inspired by a wonderful choreographer I know here in the South East of England. She is a fireball, and has met her match in Aidan.

I hope you enjoy reading this book—and I promise there are no horrid scenes that make you feel you need to drop and give anyone twenty of anything! It's just pure indulgence.

Enjoy!

*Annie O'*

# ONE NIGHT...
# WITH HER BOSS

BY
ANNIE O'NEIL

First published in Great Britain 2016
By Mills & Boon, an imprint of HarperCollins*Publishers*
1 London Bridge Street, London, SE1 9GF

Large Print edition 2016

© 2016 Annie O'Neil

ISBN: 978-0-263-26107-3

Our policy is to use papers that are natural, renewable
and recyclable products and made from wood grown
in sustainable forests. The logging and manufacturing
processes conform to the legal environmental
regulations of the country of origin.

Printed and bound in Great Britain
by CPI Antony Rowe, Chippenham, Wiltshire

**Annie O'Neil** spent most of her childhood with her leg draped over the family rocking chair and a book in her hand. Novels, baking and writing too much teenage angst poetry ate up most of her youth. Now Annie splits her time between corralling her husband into helping her with their cows, baking, reading, barrel racing (not really!), and spending some very happy hours at her computer, writing.

Find out more about Annie at her website: www.annieoneilbooks.com.

### Books by Annie O'Neil

### Mills & Boon Medical Romance

*The Surgeon's Christmas Wish*
*The Firefighter to Heal Her Heart*
*Doctor...to Duchess?*

Visit the Author Profile page at millsandboon.co.uk for more titles.

This book is for my former editor,
Charlotte Mursell, who first brought me on
board with Mills & Boon and helped fine-
tune me into the work in progress I am today
(which is better than when she got me).
This was the final book we worked on together
and she was pure inspiration. I was a lucky
gal to have begun my writing career with her.
Thank you, Charlotte!!! Annie X

# CHAPTER ONE

ALI SCRUNCHED HER eyes as tightly as she could
manage, then popped them open. Nope. No good.
Even the snow-capped stadium filled to the brim
with cheering rugby fans couldn't help her push
*That Night* back to the inaccessible recesses of
her memory. Who would've thought a liaison two
weeks ago at an airport hotel would still be sending heated shivers of response careering round
her body?

Fourteen days on and the sensations were just
as potent. She'd wanted change—and now she
was virtually swimming in it. Ali rubbed at
her arms as if that would help scrub the heated
thoughts away. *Pah!*

"Doc!" One of the players started doing star
jumps on the sidelines. "You cold? Just do some
of these—they'll warm you up sharpish."

Ali tossed a smile at the player and made a little
jog-in-place movement to show willing. She was

"only" a locum up here, but the lads had already made her feel a welcome part of the beast that was the North Stars rugby team. She wondered what it would be like when the Chief Medical Officer got back from his holiday. She was used to running her own clinic, so being someone's subordinate would take a bit of a mental shift. But learning from a master of sports medicine? That would be worth it. Definitely.

After that...who knew what lay ahead? Going back to En Pointe Physio didn't appeal. She wasn't sure if it ever would. The day she'd walked into her favorite coffee shop back in London and hadn't even needed to open her mouth to order her specialty mocha was the day she'd started hunting for a locum position. She didn't do predictable. She didn't do steady. The longer you stuck around somewhere, the more likely you were to get hurt. When you tried new things— like an unexpected one-night stand on the eve of your new job—suffice it to say, it shook things up a bit.

A shiver rippled up her spine, and even though it was pretty obvious the snowy weather had sent the chill she couldn't resist closing her eyes again.

Letting go of that night was near impossible. Especially when her body was still responding to the memory of his caresses, smoothing and shifting along her bare skin. His name...? A mystery—and it would stay that way.

Whatever had possessed them to head up to her hotel room that night—both of them with their flights grounded for a measly three inches of snow—had been well worth it. Who was she kidding? She knew *exactly* what had possessed them. Pure as the driven snow, hot as molten lava: desire. Her first ever one-night stand and it had been about as smokin' hot as they got.

The roars and songs of the crowd blurred into white noise as she dipped and dived into the ten hours and forty-seven minutes they had spent together. And on Valentine's Day, to boot! She was normally a cynic when it came to twittering birds and love hearts. Life had shown her there was no such thing as "The One." Even so, the universe must've had other ideas—at least for that one night.

"Cupid shot your plane down?" He had placed his drink on the bar next to her empty glass.

Cheesy line—but from the quirk in his lips he'd known it.

Her attraction to him had been immediate.

"That obvious?" she'd shot back with a laugh and a smile.

The bartender had placed a fresh cocktail in front of her. One she hadn't ordered. A Cosmopolitan, complete with a twist of orange peel. Her favorite.

She wasn't normally a sucker for a well-dressed man—but this one...? No matter what had been about to play out there, she'd already known she would remember him as "The Suit."

He'd worn his as if he had been sewn into it. And she hadn't doubted for a second how delicious he would look out of it.

"Been here long?"

She'd felt him make the visual journey up from her biker-style boots, crossed at the ankle, to the bit of leg on show below the swing of fabric that had made up her wraparound dress.

"Long enough."

Already, she'd only had eyes for him, and the buzz of magnetic energy had tugged them into a cocoon of "Me and You." Another sip of Cosmo, remarkably little chit-chat, a slight lift of his eyebrow—*shall we?*—and they had headed off to the elevators.

It had been raw animal attraction. They hadn't needed to discuss it. They'd just *known*. No names. No deep and meaningful forays into the other's psyche. Just unreserved, unadulterated, lust. She'd never felt anything consume her so completely before.

The doors of the elevator had barely shut before his hands had begun exploring her, heated kisses had drawn them closer together. She'd felt reckless, wanton, and exactly where she should have been. She'd been completely under his spell, and this total stranger had made himself at home with the dips and curves of her body. Fingers had slipped along waistlines, hands had been drawn possessively along hips, lips had tasted and teased and all she'd been able to do was respond.

She didn't even remember how they'd got to her room. But Ali could distinctly recall the moment her dress had slipped to the floor, her skin shuddering with desire as she'd pressed against him, still wearing every bit of that three-piece suit. She should have felt vulnerable, exposed. But she hadn't. Far from it. She'd felt feminine, sexy, and for the very first time she'd understood the power of desire.

The need to feel him inside her had grown as his hands had begun to explore her more intimately. Her breasts, then her nipples had grown taut as she'd pressed against the wool of his suit jacket. He'd slid a hand between her legs, his fingers slipping slowly back and forth, back and forth. Her breath had caught in her throat and he'd tipped his head down to lazily tease his tongue round first one nipple, then the other.

She'd rolled her feet up onto tiptoe. Fluidly, as if she were still dancing and the accident had never happened, she'd tucked first one leg and then, with a small hop, the other around his hips. He had easily carried her across the room to the high bed. As he'd begun to lower her swiftly, almost brusquely, he had turned her around, his hands moving along the sides of her breasts. Then one hand had traced along her front and the other down her back, until he'd cupped her between her legs. Her skin had felt as though it were on fire.

She had never wanted anyone more than she'd wanted The Suit.

She'd felt his thick five o'clock shadow along her cheek and, as if he reading her mind, he'd whispered into her ear, "I only have two—so you're going to have to be patient."

Two condoms. One night with a man she'd never see again.

*These walls better have soundproofing,* she remembered thinking. She'd met her match, and from the way his hands had taken such pleasure in exploring her body he'd felt it, too...

"Woooo-hoooo! Did you see that, Doc?"

Ali snapped out of her sexy dreamscape, eyes scanning the field to quickly connect the dots. *Must pay more attention!*

The clutch of assistant coaches she'd stationed herself next to were whooping it up as the scoreboard flickered to life with a new set of numbers. The North Stars were surging ahead of their opponents.

She grinned and pulled her knitted team skullcap down over her ears. Man, it was cold out here! A far cry from her swish and well-heated therapy center in the heart of London.

The thought pleased and stung at the same time. *Enough.*

The Chief Medical Officer was due back some-time today—possibly even mid-match—and it would hardly do for her to be caught daydream-ing. Especially dreams of the super-naughty kind.

She forced herself to be alert to the players on the pitch. They were, after all, her responsibility.

As play recommenced, then abruptly stopped, Ali's senses sharpened. The crunch of shoul-der on shoulder, skull on skull was never a nice sound, but these rugby boys didn't do things by halves.

The howls of pain coming from the field set her into motion. Drama queens, maybe—but these men were not babies. A player was hurting.

Oblivious to the roar of the thousands of fans watching the heated North versus South trial match, Ali picked up her pace as the stretcher-bearers joined her on the snow-spackled field. A scrum combined with a slippery playing surface could easily lead to a spinal injury. She hoped for the player's sake it wasn't the case.

The huddle of sweaty, mud-covered men split open as she arrived.

"Hope you've got a strong stomach, Harty," One of the players mumbled as she made it to the center of the group.

There, lying on the ground, staring straight ahead as he fought to control his breathing, was Chris Trace—the team's hooker. To say he was a sight to behold was putting it mildly. She almost had to laugh. She'd wanted a change and this was most definitely *not* the sort of injury you saw in the Royal Ballet.

Their player had taken the full brunt of a Southern Cross player's might. Blood was pouring from a gash in his forehead, and as he swept a hand across his face to clear it from his eyes it looked as though he was going to have one heck of a shiner by the end of play.

The stadium fell into a hush as both teams stood at attention—waiting for the verdict.

"All right, Chris." Ali grabbed her run bag and pulled out some wipes. "Let's see what price you've paid for victory."

Spitting out his mouth guard, the athlete tried to grin up at her. A good sign.

"I'll be back on the field in no time, Doc. Just put a plaster or something on me and I'll be good to go." Chris couldn't stop the flinch crossing his broad face as he tried to lift his head.

"No, you don't!" Ali pressed him back down to the ground. "You're not going anywhere until I check you out. What happened to your goggles?"

She smiled down at him, admiring his determination to finish the game. The North Stars were grittily committed to being at the fore of the infamous North against South showdown in just over three months' time. The last day of her contract. Losing a player to an injury was the last thing they needed.

She began sponging the blood off his forehead to see how big a gash they were dealing with. Head injuries were big bleeders, and with all the sprawling around in the muck these guys did infection was easy to come by.

"Goggles popped off when I landed on my face—or someone's foot knocked them. Can't remember."

"Can't remember or can't think straight?" a male voice asked from behind her.

Ali froze. She knew that voice. It had whispered deliciously naughty intentions into her ear not so very long ago.

Her eyes moved along the ground from where she knelt with Chris, her breath caught tight in her chest. Blood began to thunder between her ears as a pair of leather shoes came into view and walked to the opposite side of Chris. It was all she could do not to cry out as the owner of the shoes came into view as he kneeled across from her. *Oh, she knew him, all right.* She knew him intimately. And she didn't know him at all.

As their eyes met Ali physically felt the breath being sucked out of her body.

*The Suit.*

Images flickered past her mind's eye, of their bodies tangled together in a series of sexual acrobatics she'd never believed possible. A wash of pleasure rippled through her and it was all she could do to keep her jaw clamped firmly shut.

She'd never asked him his real name. Nor had he of her. That had been their deal. One night only.

*Someone needed to pinch her. And fast.*

"Take me through it."

He was speaking to her, but looking at Chris. *What was he doing here?*

"I want to find my goggles." Chris tried to push up from the ground again.

"No, you don't!"

"No, you don't!"

Ali could barely suppress a surprised smile as she and The Suit each pressed on a shoulder, keeping Chris on the ground.

"Not until we know what else you've done to yourself. How does the socket around your eye feel?" Ali pressed him down again, this time with her hands covered in purple nitrile gloves, before she gently palpated the area.

"Fine—it's just the cut, Doc. Honestly. Dr. Tate—tell her."

For a second time Ali felt her chest constrict.

"*You're* Aidan Tate?"

Dr. Aidan Tate? The award-winning sports medicine expert whose articles on non-surgical sports injuries she'd devoured like chocolate? The North Stars' Chief Medical Officer? And...wait for it...*her new boss*?

*Well.* This was a bit of a pickle.

The biggest freaking pickle in the whole entire universe!

Her tummy pirouetted and heated as she stared

at him—only just managing to suppress a smile. A short, sharp shake shifted the X-rated images from her mind and she rapidly went back to swabbing away the blood from Chris's forehead.

"Earth to Lockhart! *Harty?* What gives? Am I getting back into play or what? *Where are my goggles?*" he shouted to the other players, who leapt into action.

Ali looked up and caught the eyes of her new boss. His face was unreadable. Hmm… This was nothing short of awkward.

"Got 'em!" One of the Southern Cross players jogged over and handed the protective eyewear to Chris, complete with blood and a tuft of muddy grass. He plopped them on the front of his blood-smeared face and gave Ali a *See? I'm Fine* grin.

"Nice look, Chris." Ali guffawed at the grue-somely comic sight, then looked across at Aidan Tate with a mortified expression. He was her new boss. Never mind that she'd seen him naked. He'd hired her to be a *doctor*, not to snicker at the play-ers' made-for-Halloween gruesome faces.

*Way to make an impression, Lockhart.*

She was surprised to see Aidan smirk his ap-proval at her reaction to Chris. She guessed he wanted to make sure the new girly doc could play gross with the rest of the boys.

She glanced at Aidan again, and he nodded for her to proceed. She couldn't help but feel whatever she said was going to be under microscopic examination. Which was fair enough. If she'd found out the man she'd had a sizzling one-night stand with was her shiny new employee she would probably have held him to a higher standard.

"The cut doesn't look too deep. Let's do the spine and concussion drills and then get you to the sidelines for a couple of stitches." Then for good measure she added, "And maybe give your specs a bit of a bath."

Ali trained her eyes on Chris and deftly carried out a thorough inspection of his neck and upper spine to make sure it was safe to move him.

"Any tingling sensations in your arms? Burning? Stinging?" She rattled through the checklist, all too aware of Aidan's eyes on her.

"Nah," Chris answered.

"Shortness of breath?" She tapped along his lungs. A pneumothorax would be an unwelcome complication.

Chris heaved in a deep breath of air and exhaled with a lion noise. His lungs were fine. "Nope."

"Guess you've kept everything intact except your brainbox—lucky boy. Wiggle your toes."

"I'm *fine*, Harty! We're a breed apart from all your fluffy ballerinas. Made of tougher stuff, we are."

"Oh, really? And here was me thinking you were only human." She signaled to the stretcher lads. He was safe to move off the field for a more thorough consultation.

"No way!" Chris pushed himself up. "I'm walking off on my own two feet, thank you very much."

He stood up between them—weaving ever so slightly—then raised his arms in a victory move and swaggered off the field to the roar of the crowd.

Which left her face-to-face with Dr. Aidan Tate.

Her stomach gave a life-affirming heave and she almost lost her balance, which—considering she was still kneeling—was quite a feat. The man took her breath away. There was no getting away from that. Salt and pepper hair she'd run her fingers through on their way to naughtier climes, coffee-black eyes and a perfect set of cheekbones. Oh—and had she mentioned his lips? They were very, *very* nice lips.

"Go on." He pointed toward the sidelines, pushing up to a standing position. "You've got work to do."

She rose and looked into his eyes—hoping for some answers to the thousands of questions whirling round her head, well aware that every part of her body was responding to seeing him again. Hearing him. Being close enough to touch him.

"You need to leave the pitch so all that stops."

"What?" She looked around.

He lifted his chin in the direction of the stands, from where a flow of catcalls was pealing out. They were obviously aimed at Ali.

"You're fine with that?" Aidan's dark eyes crackled—the energy between them was as potent as it had been the first time they'd met.

"The shouting?"

"Yes." His face was grim.

"I can barely hear them." And it was the truth.

All her senses were triangulating in one very specific direction.

"I'm not fine with it." Aidan took her by the elbow, turned her around and began to walk her off the field.

"Hey! I can walk on my own, thank you very much!" Ali protested.

"You don't need to make a bigger show of things than you already have," Aidan bit out.

"I'm sorry?" Ali bridled. "I think the only 'show' was Chris's head-bleed. Frog-marching me off the field is a pretty bad idea."

And it was. Aidan dropped her elbow instantly and strode off the field. She could make her own way.

Dr. A. Lockhart. Dance injury specialist, sports medicine MD, and surgeon, brought in for a locum position. When he'd hired her he'd thought her ream of credentials made her perfect for fine-tuning the team's training in the build-up to the final.

And now he knew she was very same woman who had slowly but surely been consuming every sane brain cell he had left since their night at the airport?

Miss Cosmopolitan.

She had actually rocked his world. Never before had a woman made such an impression on him. From the very moment he'd laid eyes on her.

She'd been sitting at the hotel bar, her eyes on the television weather report, lazily tracing a swizzle stick along her lips. He had become mesmerized by the movement as her mouth had responded to the touch of the little black straw. It had been just about the sexiest thing he'd thought he'd ever seen. Before he could give himself time to think better of it he'd sent her a drink. Ten...fifteen minutes couldn't have passed before they'd been in the elevator and he'd been tracing a finger along her lips, hungry for more. *Much* more.

No names...no attachments. It wasn't how he normally operated—had ever operated—but by the time they had been finished she had been worth every single nail scratch on his back.

He narrowed his eyes as he watched her disappear down the tunnel toward the changing rooms. Glossy black hair streaming in a thick swatch from beneath her team cap, crystal-clear blue eyes so bright they seemed lit from within, and a pair of raspberry-red lips which he could all too easily remember—

*No you don't! Stop.*

"Doc! Watch it!"

Aidan nearly collided with Chris, who was trying to give his face a scrub with his filthy jersey.

"Sorry, mate. Away with the fairies."

"Where's Harty?" Chris looked around the sidelines.

"Who?"

"Dr. Lockhart," Chris bit out, his tone abruptly changing.

"Chris, are you all right?" Aidan walked him over to a bench.

Ali had capably gone through the concussion test, he knew—he'd kept careful watch. But sometimes a clot could appear later, with devastating effect. He hoped that wasn't the case.

"Yeah, fine." Chris exhaled heavily as he sat. "I just want to get back out there. When's Harty going to stitch me up?"

"Don't you trust my stitches anymore?" As the words came out of his mouth Aidan knew they sat wrong, but the mention of Dr. Lockhart on such comfortable, friendly terms had riled him.

She'd been here—what?—a fortnight?—and already had a nickname? He'd been with the team five years and had barely managed to get the odd "Doc" out of the players. Then again—it wasn't exactly as if he was the easiest person to get to know. He knew if he was more open with the players they would respond in kind—but he wasn't there yet. Maybe he never would be. Maybe "closed off" was just who he was.

Either way—he didn't need to be behaving like a jealous doctor. Ali's stitches...his stitches—it didn't matter. She was a highly qualified doctor and he'd hired her for her skills. She clearly had the stomach for it. A "fluffy ballerina" type wouldn't laugh at a face covered in blood. The best thing he could do was shake it all off. It would keep things professional. Unlike his response to Ali.

Feeling envious because the players got along with the new doctor...? Ridiculous. It was what anyone would hope for. Harmony between support staff and players.

He scraped a hand along his stubbled jawline. *Harmony?*

Who was he kidding? The only way he could

describe his response to Ali Lockhart was Class A caveman. And that wasn't going to work. Not here. His reputation went hand in hand with the team's. Work and emotions weren't things he mixed. *Ever.* His annual fortnight of charity work in the Pacific Islands was an upfront-and-center reminder of that. Five years on and he still hadn't shed a tear. Maybe he never would.

"Are you all right for me to do the stitches?"

Ali appeared by his side with a suture kit in her hands.

"Go ahead." He nodded in Chris's direction without looking at her. Those blue eyes spoke volumes and he couldn't go there. Not now. "Do the concussion tests again before you okay him for play."

"Would you rather do it?"

"You're getting paid to look after these boys. You go on ahead."

He kept his eyes on the field, arms tightly crossed over his chest as he watched the players get into formation at the referee's whistle. It might look like mayhem to some, but he liked rugby. There was a system. A playbook. Rules.

He liked order, and Ali's presence here was bringing nothing but chaos.

Ali wished she could scrub away the crimson heat racing into her cheeks. She wasn't used to being spoken to like an underling.

The cheek! Her hands flew to her face. *Her* cheeks! *Aaaargh!*

She huffed out a sigh and started swabbing at Chris's mud- and blood-covered forehead.

Working with Britain's premier sports physician was meant to be professionally rewarding. *Trying* was more like it! On multiple levels.

"Ouch! Easy, Harty."

"I thought you were a roughtie-toughtie?" Ali gave Chris an apologetic grin and tried to lighten her touch.

She couldn't let Aidan get to her. Not on a professional front, anyway. Her job was the one thing Ali knew she excelled at, and she was not about to let some perfectly gorgeous chippy doctor from up here in the hinterlands boss her about. Even if she *had* spent several hot and steamy, never to be repeated, perfectly delicious hours of lovemaking with him.

She rubbed a numbing agent on Chris's forehead, quickly put in the stiches and gave him another run through the concussion exam. She wasn't one hundred percent convinced—not enough to prove to Aidan, anyway—so told him he'd have to sit out the rest of the game, and then she'd do the tests again.

"Safety first!" she quipped with a Doris Day grin. Or at least that was the look she was going for. Chris stuck his tongue out at her in response. Child…

Maybe coming here had been a mistake. Already she was getting attached to these big old lugheads, and that hadn't been part of the plan. Not by a long shot. Nor had sleeping with her new boss, but it seemed that had happened, too. This was all going swimmingly!

Aidan Tate was The Suit.

Who would've believed it?

She'd been a secret admirer of his expertise for years. He'd sounded so caring and professional in the medical journals he was regularly published in. And he'd been oh, so very tender and attentive at three, four *and* five in the morning, when neither of them had felt the need to sleep. Humph! *Double*-humph!

She grabbed her phone from her coat pocket and did what she always did when things started to get emotional. She bashed out a message to her former mentor from dance school.

What's the protocol on breaking my contract?

Her mentor had been wise and sage, had had hair like Einstein and—also like Einstein—he had known everything. At least about her. The one person on the planet who had. He'd helped her move on. Just as she had when her mum had died. Just as she had when she had learned she would never dance again.

Then she deleted it. He was gone now—some ten years ago—and she wasn't a quitter. Never had been. Except when life had forced her to... to alter her course. That was how she preferred to see things. Taking matters into her own hands.

She took her cap off and ran her hand through her hair. Platitudes. Handy when you needed them, trite when you didn't.

She tried to focus on the stands, the players, the flashing billboards—anything to keep her eyes from the unmoving figure of Aidan Tate. But no matter where she looked her internal camera kept imposing Aidan everywhere. On the big screens, on the looping advertising banners encircling the pitch...even the close-ups of the players showed those flashing dark eyes and that thick black hair she'd so enjoyed running her fingers through as she—*ahem*—had behaved distinctly unlike her old self.

Aidan had quite obviously been behaving out of character, as well. Caring and studious? *Ha!* Cranky control freak was more like it. It appeared looks weren't the only things that could be deceiving.

She tipped her head back and forth in the hope that some answers might fall out. If she'd learned anything in the past few years, it was that most situations were definitely *not* what they seemed to be. She needed to get out of there.

She watched as the players hurled themselves around the field.

No.

She didn't.

She owed it to these guys to stick around.

She'd made an oath. An oath to protect and care

for her patients. And there they were—all cauliflower ears, biceps bulging, thigh muscles like logs, all gussied up in their unmistakable red-and-black uniforms. The North Stars.

As the cool air swirled around her play intensified and the crowd audibly kept pace with the action. She couldn't have felt further away from home. Not that she had one to go back to anyhow. Which was the whole point, wasn't it? Being here. Now.

*The past is where it belongs,* she reminded herself. *You're safe here.*

Ali couldn't help letting a burble of giggles escape her lips. Safe here? On the sidelines of one of Britain's most brutal games?

That'd be about right.

# CHAPTER TWO

SWITCHING ON THE overhead lights to her warehouse loft flat, Ali felt the adrenaline from the day's match drain away. The adrenaline from finding out The Suit was her new boss…? *That* little nugget was keeping her pulse-rate a bit high.

She kicked off her shoes. They landed one by one with a satisfying thunk-thunk on the far side of the flat. She was giving "bachelorette pad messy" a whirl, and it was fun. More fun than watching Aidan sort out the day's steady stream of cuts, abrasions and strained muscles. She thought she'd earned some Brownie points with her treatment of Chris's cut, but he'd hardly let her so much as swab a skinned knee after that. So much for earning her keep…

Her stores of controlled breathing, counting to ten and biting her tongue had pretty much been exhausted by the time the final whistle had blown.

Where was the amazing physician she'd heard about, who took new doctors under his wing and single-handedly teased new and seemingly un-reachable skills out of them? Where was the vol-unteer coach lauded as a hero to a rugby squad of twelve-year-old girls? Who had stolen the doctor every medical journal in Britain couldn't praise enough and replaced him with Generalissimo Grumpyhead? What was the point of being here if she wasn't going to *learn* anything?

She leaned against the closed door, well aware that her body was virtually vibrating with all the things she had learned from him—just nothing she could use in the workplace.

*But honestly!* Who in their right mind would turn down a guy who looked as if he could fix your car, fend off a swath of marauding invaders and pose for one of those posters of sexy guys holding tires in a garage, wearing not much more than a scrappy old pair of jeans? Scrappy jeans just slipping off his hips...right where the little notchy muscle definition bits met...

*Nooooooo! Not* the way this thought process was meant to go.

She felt herself soften. A little. He couldn't be

*that* much of a control freak. She had just worked two weeks on her own while he'd been off swanning around in the Pacific, or wherever it was they said he'd gone. Maybe it was all part of some unknown test he set for his minions. Prove thyself—then watch and learn.

Geniuses were supposed to be arrogant, condescending, haughty and superior—but from what she'd read this guy had sounded as if he had heart. That would need some excavating. Not to mention his inability to give her a go. He should be thanking his lucky stars she had come up here at all! She had her own reams of kudos, accrued over a lifetime of—well, of avoiding everything one did in life but work.

*Bah!* None of this was helping.

She padded across the worn Oriental rug sprawled across the aged wood floors. It was the only thing she'd brought from her "old life" in London, and it matched the vintage feel of the building perfectly. The floor-to-ceiling windows were her favorite feature of the loft. A classic accent from the building's heyday as a thread factory. If she was really honest she could very easily fall in love with the place. An enormous loft penthouse with an enviable view overlooking the River Teal versus her two-up, two-down with a view across the street? It'd be pretty easy to get used to this.

Not that the flat was her new *home*. It was an investment. She didn't put down roots. She made investments. Easier to leave that way.

Ali slipped her keys into a red-lacquered bowl she'd found at a charity shop—the only decorative touch to her kitchen island—and pulled open the door to her enormous American-style refrigerator. The pickings were pretty sparse. The remains of a triangle of cheddar, an out of date ready-to-bake baguette and some just-about-to-wilt salad greens were the only inhabitants of the shelves. It was hardly the food of champions.

She had hit the ground running when she'd moved up here, and grocery shopping hadn't made it on to her list of things to do. After such a rough day, a hot meal would go down a treat. In London she'd already be on the phone, ordering Thai noodles or a delicious eggplant parmigiana from Casa de Luna. They made it perfectly—crispy round the edges, nice and gooey in the center. Here—well, she knew they had takeaways, up here in the wilds of the North of England, but...

It wasn't the same.

"It's *not* the same—and that's the point, you ninny," she scolded herself out loud. Onward and upward!

She was here to push her limits, to reach new horizons and blah-dee-blah-blah-blah. How many pep talks did she have to give herself before something, somewhere, felt right again?

Heaving a dramatic sigh, Ali draped her team duffel coat over one of the two kitchen bar stools, went to her bedroom, peeled off the layers of outdoor gear and put on her favorite pajama shorts with a cozy slouch-shouldered jumper.

*Me, some scraps of old cheese and a bit of TV. Precisely what the doctor ordered!*

The jangle of the doorbell nearly made her jump out of her skin. She hadn't had any visitors before and certainly wasn't expecting any now.

She hurriedly pulled on her woolly slipper boots and jogged to the door. When she pulled it open her stomach careened round her insides and her heart lurched into her throat all in one blood-racing moment.

Standing there, or rather filling up her doorway, eyes twinkling and a bottle of red dangling from his fingers, was The Suit.

"Hello, there, neighbor. Fancy a bit of work talk over a glass of *vino*?"

Ali's heart changed its syncopation—moving from dirge to dance mix in an instant. Pure determination kept her from unleashing a broad smile at his presence. She was a steely-gazed doctor, not a moony-eyed teenager. *Right?*

Her body's response to Aidan had absolutely nothing to do with the fact that he was the most gorgeous male specimen she'd ever seen. Clothed or otherwise. Or with the fact that his voice was about as trickle-down-your-spine scrumptious as they came. Especially when he was whispering sweet nothings into her ear as he traced his fingers across her bare belly in an endless swirl of figure-eights.

He was an arrogant know-it-all! And now he was her *neighbor*?

"What are you doing here?"

Not really a comment out of the etiquette books, but she was pretty sure they were past social niceties.

"I live a couple of buildings down in the complex and thought I'd be a bit more welcoming than I was this afternoon," he explained with an innocent smile.

"But how did you know I…?" she started, then petered out.

"Apart from the fact your contact details are listed on every emergency sheet at the stadium, who do you think sent you the recommendation you check the place out?" He held up the bottle of red. "This was my thank-you from the building committee for your decision to move in. I thought it would only be fair to share the spoils."

Aidan practically purred as he made to enter her apartment minus an invitation.

Ali stepped aside on autopilot, all too aware of the scrummy male scent of him as he swept past her into the loft. She could think of a thing or two he could do to be more welcoming—and they were definitely not in an etiquette book.

*Regroup!* Ali stared at the closed door and tried to come up with a plan. *Think, think, think, think.*

*Kick him out. It's the only way. Time to show the upper hand.*

Ali whirled around, only to see Aidan merrily nosing around her kitchen.

"What's for dinner, honey? Hope it goes with red!"

Aidan's voice was infused with the same twinkle of humor she could see in his eyes. The same rascally voice that had kidded her about how quickly she had managed to rip his clothes off. Well, not *rip* exactly—she had been aware that he might need his shirt the next day—but who knew cotton could seem such a thick barrier between a woman and The Suit's chest? The clothes had had to go!

He gave her a wink. A cute one that threatened the tightly pinched corners of her mouth. He really *did* have the most beautiful brown eyes. They somehow managed to look even more like dark chocolate now than they had the first time she'd seen them. A rich contrast to the deep maroon lambswool jumper that his shoulders filled to designer perfection. Of course. Would The Suit's shoulders do anything but?

What had happened to his suit, anyway? Probably best he didn't have it on. Too much temptation. Mind you, his earth-toned moleskin trousers didn't exactly look off the rack. Aidan was rocking a sophisticated "lad" look. Complete with ironically arched eyebrow as he scanned her flat.

It was obvious, as she watched him take in the old leather sofa, the bare walls and the small dining table without chairs, that he found her living arrangements amusing.

"I'm presuming no one told you we have furniture stores up here?"

"Look—" Ali started, then clamped her lips tight. It wasn't as if she was going to tell him she'd sold all of her furniture in a spontaneous and very thorough need to clutter-clear.

Everything she'd had before her mum died was a memory, and ever since then she didn't do rehashes of the past. She wasn't going to tell him a single thing. Not about her mother. Not about her who-knew-where-the-hell-he-was? father. Not about the accident that had ended her dance career before it had even begun. Not a word. Just like she'd said at the airport. No names. No history. Just unbridled passion.

It was obvious Aidan wasn't after a roll in the hay now. He was on a fact-finding mission.

Too bad! This was *her* space. One night stands

at snowy airports were one thing. Casual drop-
in dinner dates with her grouch of a boss had a
whole other rulebook.

"Doesn't seem the doctor's got much in the
house."

Aidan was making himself quite at home—
merrily inspecting her refrigerator's stores and,
having found them wanting, opening up the
cupboard doors where he would see, Ali knew,
absolutely no food. It was all very familiar for
someone with whom she was—er—intimately
familiar.

"I've been busy. I haven't really—"

"If you're going to be part of this team you've
got to keep your energy up." Aidan wagged a
teasing finger in her direction.

Who *was* this man? Dr. Jolly-Jekyll or Mr.
Keep-Your-Hands-Off Hyde?

"Well?" Aidan looked at her expectantly.

"Sorry? I didn't catch that." Ali tugged her fingers through her hair, twisting a few dark strands
round her index finger. Her stomach was in knots,
so her hair might as well be, too.

"What's it short for?"

"What?" She stared at him blankly.

"Your full name—I presume it's not Ali."

"Alexis. Defender of humankind," she answered by rote, eyes suddenly locked with his.

Aidan stepped out from behind the kitchen bar, clasping her right hand between both of his. A burst of electricity shot along her spine as she found herself eye to eye with the appealing expanse of his chest. She'd kissed that chest. Lots. A nice display of sexy man whorls of hair above a *c'mon, punch me hard* set of abs.

If she were to look up into those espresso-colored eyes of his and—

She felt her hand being rigorously shaken.

*Er... Was she missing something here?*

"Hello there, Alexis." He further corrected himself, "Dr. Lockhart. I think we got off to the wrong start today."

*Today?*

"Allow me to introduce myself. I'm Dr. Aidan Tate, Chief Medical Officer for the North Stars—at your service."

He dropped her tingling fingers, took a broad step backward and performed a half bow, then looked up at her with those incredible, endlessly dark eyes. Ali felt her knees give a little.

*For heaven's sake. You've met the entire royal family and didn't act like such a ninny. Pull yourself together!*

She gave him a slight head-nod. If this was his version of an apology he had yet to win her over. Well. Professionally. "Dr. Ali Lockhart—at *your* service."

There were a number of things Aidan could have said in response, but they wouldn't serve the purpose of his visit. He was here to begin afresh with Dr. Alexis Lockhart, the team's new physio-surgeon with one turn-you-green-with-envy CV.

"On paper it looks as though you've never taken a moment off to do anything other than study or practice medicine. When did you start? When you were twelve?"

"Something like that." Ali crossed her arms protectively across her chest and looked away.

There was a story there. Maybe too much time in the science lab accounted for her wild-girl antics at the airport.

His gaze slipped down toward Ali's feet, stopping to note a couple of scars on her left knee. He'd not noticed them the other night—which was pretty amazing, considering the gymnastics they had achieved. His curiosity was piqued, but he looked away. He wasn't being fair. He'd come here to apologize and now he was treating her just the way he'd insisted to the coach the players would. Like chattel.

Coach Stone had been fairly terse when Aidan had suggested they see if they could transfer her to another team and bring in a different locum for the rest of the tournament season. One who wasn't so easy on the eyes.

"Not a chance." That had been the unwavering reply. The players had taken to her straight away, Stone had said, and hiring someone else with credentials like hers at this point in the season was going to be nigh on impossible. She was staying and that was that.

He cleared his throat and looked at Ali's reflection in the window. *Since when were lambswool boots and a mismatched set of pajamas so sexy?*

Maybe if he pictured Ali with an eye patch it would help. And a hideous perm. And a hunchback.

"Earth to Aidan?" Ali was waving her hands in front of his face, pulling him out of an embarrassingly obvious stupor.

"Yeah—sorry, I was just thinking."

"Anything you care to share?"

*Might as well go for it.*

"The elephant in the room."

"Which elephant would that be?" Ali smiled her hostess smile at him.

Aidan couldn't help returning her smile. If things were different they'd make a great pair. But they weren't—so it was best to lay his cards on the table. The man she'd met at the airport didn't exist in his everyday life. The man she'd met was an anomaly.

"Well, we could talk about the big elephant— about how we slept together—or the smaller one—how you should probably clear your spare underwear and gym kit out of my desk."

"Oh, blimey. That's *your* desk, is it?" Ali clapped her hands over her mouth.

"Who else's would it be?"

"I don't know—it didn't seem to have anything personal on it so I just thought it was free."

*Good point.* He didn't do personal. Especially at work. But that didn't address the issue at hand.

"The locker rooms have eyes and ears, Dr. Lockhart. Very acutely tuned, testosterone-charged cauliflower ears. I don't think it would be wise to have what happened at the airport being public knowledge. Or to be repeated."

She gulped, looked away, then began to laugh. Nervous giggles or happy memories? He knew what camp *he* was in.

"Can you imagine if the lads knew?" she asked. "About that night?" she qualified, as if he could have even begun to forget.

She lifted her gaze to his and this time he was certain they both felt the same connection. Having her standing in front of him in sexy little jim-jams wasn't strictly helping his body keep it neutral.

Her expression turned sober. "You're right. Absolutely right. The only reason I came up here was to learn, and all the..." she blew a slow breath between her lips "...other stuff would just get in the way."

They nodded at each other for a moment, as if they'd just signed a significant pact. And they had. They would be colleagues only. It was agreed.

"I know it wasn't what you planned for tonight—but what do you say we go out for a bite to eat?"

Ali gave him a dubious look.

"To talk about the team...your next three months here and what you hope to get out of it. Professionally." He weighted the word as a reminder to himself.

"I'd like that," she replied, then looked down at her skimpy outfit. "I'm guessing pajamas aren't the dress code. Smart or casual?"

He knew what he wanted to say, but picked the pragmatic response. As agreed. "Casual is fine. I know a great little Greek place—just around the corner."

"Love a bit of meze!" Her smile brightened. "Give me two minutes."

He smiled at Ali's retreating figure. The man who she'd met at the airport would have waited as long as she needed. Not that he'd tell her that. This whole situation was a matter of using his head over his...other parts. They'd had their night and it had been a one-off. Now he just had to work his way through the next one-hundred-odd days, convincing himself that all work and no play was the most sensible thing to do.

He'd made it through the past five years without so much as a fissure in his heart. Keeping Ali at arm's length couldn't be that hard. What was the worst that could happen?

Operation Pals-R-Us was officially under way.

"Are you kidding me? It came out of the *socket*?" Ali could barely contain her disbelief. She was really going to have to hone her shoulder joint skills. Knees...? She had them nailed. Shoulders...? Not so commonly injured during the *pas de deux*.

"Completely. You could've heard his screams down in London, I'll bet—but I got it back in, he's been diligent with his rehab, and now to see Mack run you'd never know otherwise."

"Amazing. To get him playing again was quite a feat." Ali didn't bother curbing her *I'm impressed* voice as she put her serviette onto her empty plate. Bodies were crazy things, and it sounded like Aidan had had his fair share of having to think outside the box to keep his players fit.

"I had to. These guys have a really short career window. If I can help make it just a little bit longer—so much the better."

She had to fight the automatic wince. *Her* career window had been just as short. *Nonexistent* was more like it. But the past was the past. The players were lucky they had someone like Aidan looking out for them.

In fact, his idea to go out to dinner had turned into a good one. Better than she'd thought when they'd first arrived at the restaurant after a virtually silent ten-minute walk. Trying to make chitchat when all you can think about is kissing your new boss was tough work.

After a bit of an awkward recitation of their professional histories, and some seriously divine moussaka with homemade pita, they had moved on to medical horror stories. The topic was inevitable between doctors, and it had definitely put the pair of them on neutral territory.

In fact, Ali discovered as the evening zipped along, it was really fun. Aidan was turning out to be everything she'd hoped when she had agreed to the locum posting. Smart, funny—and, yes, deeply gorgeous, but she hadn't known that when she'd signed on the dotted line. And now they'd agreed to keep things professional... Thank God they had medicine in common!

"I hope you don't mind—" Ali held up her hand to flag the waiter. She'd just about eaten her body weight in moussaka and was ready to crash for the night.

"Not up for a shot of ouzo?"

*Ugh.* The thought turned her stomach. "No, thanks—you're on your own with that one."

"No problem. I'm amazed I made it this late."

She raised an inquisitive eyebrow.

"Jet lag," he explained.

"Crikey! I totally forgot. You must be exhausted. Where was your holiday—some island in the Pacific, wasn't it?"

"It wasn't exactly a holiday." Tricky. Aidan wasn't one to lie—but he wasn't in the habit of letting anyone into his confidence either.

"Oh?"

"It's just something I do every year."

She looked at him blankly.

"For a charity."

"Oh, right! Which one?" Her eyes brightened.

"It's to do with the tropical storm that devastated the region a few years back."

"Oh, gosh. I remember that. It was horrible, wasn't it? Thousands of lives lost, weren't there?"

"Mmm. It took a lot of lives." Including one that had meant the world to him.

"That's brilliant that you go out there. I've often thought of doing some charity work in London—inner-city kids, that sort of thing—but I was always so wrapped up at the clinic."

"You really made a success of that, didn't you?" Aidan gratefully swerved from more questions about the island. Yes, he did charity work—but the rest of it...? That was neatly locked up in his emotional no-go zone.

"I hope so," Ali began to twist the corners of her serviette into a tight coil. "Most people thought I was foolish for opening such a specialized clinic—but it's not as if the only ballerinas who injure themselves are in the Royal Ballet. We get clients from all over the world now. My 'little baby' is all grown up now."

"You were smart. Got in there before someone else thought of it and then made an art of it."

Aidan nodded his approval—not that she needed it. En Pointe was now *the* destination for anyone with a dance-related injury. Impressive for someone who'd just turned thirty-two. The only way you could get that kind of success, this early, was undiluted drive.

"So how could you leave it all behind?"

Ali looked away.

"Oh…it was time to spread my wings—let new pairs of eyes see to things."

"So you're not going back?" This time he couldn't hide the surprise in his voice. "I don't know if I could leave *my* baby as easily."

"You mean you'd never leave the North Stars?"

"No, it's not that. If something amazing tempted me I'm sure I'd go. But I'm happy enough here, and any 'wing-stretching' I need to do lands in the clinic just about every week in the form of new injuries, new techniques. I don't need to go elsewhere. Don't get me wrong—I'm delighted you're here—but to leave behind your clinic after putting all that time and energy into it… It's your calling card, surely?"

"No," Ali answered quietly, still avoiding his gaze. "I never needed to be lauded for the work we do at En Pointe—I just wanted to make sure the resource was there. Dancers need a place they can rely on to specifically deal with *all* their needs when they're injured. That's why it provides a multi-level approach to the care it gives. We don't just stick bandages on the dancers. They receive surgery, rehab, counseling—the whole lot."

"That sounds like the voice of experience." Aidan leaned forward, lowering his head to see if she would receive his inquisitive smile.

"We've all got history." Her eyes remained resolutely elsewhere. "Shall we...?" Ali abruptly dropped her knotted serviette onto the table and briskly headed toward the waiter who'd been making up their bill.

"Hang on, Ali." Aidan jogged to catch up with her, pulling his wallet out of his pocket. "This one's on me."

"No need," she replied with a tight smile. "I'm perfectly capable of looking after myself." A look of remorse flashed across her face. "Sorry. Thank you. That's very kind." She shot him an apologetic grimace. "I guess you're not the only one who's tired."

"Not to worry."

Aidan handed a couple of bills to the waiter and waved away any change as Ali shrugged on the coat she'd left on one of the hooks near the front door. She was halfway out the door by the time he'd grabbed his own. There was definitely a story there—a painful one, from the looks of things. But he wasn't one to dig—particularly as he'd been doing his own "artful dodging." He was no psychiatrist, but he'd put money on the idea that Alexis Lockhart—defender of human-kind—hadn't come up North solely to expand her medical horizons.

"Shall we go back via the river route?"

"You're the boss!" Ali quipped.

"Hopefully not a *bossy* boss," he shot back with a grin. Witty lines had never really been his forte.

"There's still time." Her face bore no trace of humor.

Aidan chose silence as the best response. He'd had enough experience with clamping his mouth shut when yet another woman he'd casually dated had expressed disappointment over things not turning more serious. Not that Ali seemed all that interested in plumbing emotional depths with him. Quite the opposite, in fact. Keeping things superficial…? Now, *that* he could do.

She rubbed her hands together in the cold winter air and huffed out a puff of breath. "Sorry. I'm sounding really narky and I don't mean to."

He pointed her toward the riverside path that would bring them to their respective homes. And he didn't mean to be superficial. Not with her. He felt a rush of desire to keep things between them on a good level—positive. He'd already seen two sides to this woman and he liked them both. Very much.

"Not to worry. It's been a long day."

"You can say that again."

# CHAPTER THREE

"ALL RIGHT, LADS—let's clear some room for the lady." The assistant coach ushered the players aside for Ali, with her medical tote bag in hand.

"It's only *Harty*!" one of the guys shouted.

"Cheers, mate," Ali riposted.

She enjoyed being just "one of the lads." It was about a gazillion times easier than being anywhere near Aidan, whose mere presence insisted upon reminding her of how very much like a woman he had made her feel.

"What did you do this time, Rory? Eyes all right?"

She knelt down on the ground next to Rory Stiles, who was busy clutching his shoulder with his eyes squeezed tight shut. From his expression, it looked as though the blindside flanker had taken the full brunt of his fellow player's might. As she peeled his hand away from his shoulder, one glance at the tenting at his collarbone told her all she needed to know.

"Right. Let's get you off the field and into the clinic. You've done a job on your clavicle."

The redheaded athlete cracked open his eyes and tried to grin at her through the pain. "It's nothing, Harty. Just get a figure-of-eight on me and I'll see out the rest of the practice."

"No sling is going to see you through the next thirty seconds, let alone two hours, my friend." She smiled down at him. These guys were just like dancers. Injured or not—the show must go on!

"Just give me some meds—I'll be fine."

"I'm afraid I can't give you pain meds right now. Not until we know what else you've done to yourself. We want those bones to heal properly, don't we?"

"Tate would give me meds!"

"No, he wouldn't." The familiar rich voice filled the air around them. "What's going on?"

"Rory seems to have broken his collarbone and wants to compromise his long-term health for the sake of a practice session."

"No need to be so melodramatic, Dr. Lockhart.

These lads are made of sterner stuff than your tutu brigade." Aidan knelt down alongside her.

"My *what?*"

"Ah! Ha-ha-ha! Tutu brigade! Good one, Dr. Tate."

Rory laughed and Ali shot him a look. One that said, *Thanks for nothing,* and carried on with her silent and thorough inspection of Rory's neck and upper spine.

What was *that*? thought Aidan. The *fifth* time he'd stuck his foot in it today? Working with Ali was becoming progressively more difficult. Yes, he respected her professionally—but the side of him that wanted her on a completely carnal level was constantly threatening to take over his practical side. His professional side. The one he'd insisted they respect. Work. Careers. Things you could rely on. And all he could think about was taking her in his arms and having his *very* wicked way with her.

"Any tingling sensations in your arm?" Ali asked Rory.

"Nah."

"Shortness of breath?"

Rory sucked in a deep breath. "Nope."

"Guess you've kept your arteries out of the pinch zone. Lucky boy. Doesn't feel like a compound fracture—otherwise it'd be surgery for you!"

"C'mon, Rory. Up you get. I'll have a look." Aidan went to help Rory push up from the ground.

"Excuse me, I think we're good here. Aren't we, Rory?" Ali moved to Rory's other side as he rose.

"You and me are *always* good, Harty. Now...if Tate, here, would just shave a little more often—"

"Invasive surgery isn't the answer to everything." Aidan glared across the expanse of Rory's chest at her.

"I'm pretty sure I've got this one covered, Dr. Tate."

"Hey, listen, guys—no need to fight over me." Rory giggled.

"We're not fighting!" Ali and Aidan answered simultaneously.

"Uh..." Rory looked round at his teammates. "Anyone else here see Mommy and Daddy bickering again?"

"Yup."

"Sure did."

"Me too!"

"Same old, same old."

Aidan tightened his grip on Rory's elbow as the confirmations rolled in. They weren't fighting.

"Dr. Lockhart and I were merely having a professional disagreement. Over treatment. Which is a wise thing to do. Options should always be discussed before invasive action is taken. That was the reasoning behind our hiring Dr. Lockhart in the first place."

"Not because she's a hot doc?" shouted one of the boys.

Aidan threw a glance in Ali's direction, hoping for some backup. Annoyingly, she was laughing along with the rest of the lads.

"Rory. Get a move on. We need to get some ice on you and take some X-rays."

"I'll just stay here with the boys, shall I?" Ali called after him.

"Whatever you think is best, Dr. Lockhart," Aidan called over his shoulder, hating himself as he did it.

What could he do, though? It wasn't as though he was going to *admit* he had the hots for his new colleague. Work and pleasure—they just didn't mix. If it meant he had to come across as a hard-ass some of the time—well, then, so be it. These boys had a tournament to win—and that needed to be his priority.

"What was *that* all about?"

Ali held the door open, but didn't look anywhere near issuing him an invitation to enter. She hadn't said two words to him the rest of the day at work, and he couldn't blame her. He'd gone all Cro-Magnon on her and that wasn't the best way to work together. It wasn't *any* way to work together.

"Would it help if I said you were possibly right?"

"Possibly?" Ali looked indignant.

"Well, it's a fracture. I strapped him up—figure-eight—and told him to rest and ice it tonight, and that both of us would take a look in the morning, when the swelling had gone down."

"That's very magnanimous of you." Ali fake-smiled at him, then began to close the door as she spoke. "Thank you for coming by to let me know."

"*This*—" he lifted up a two grocery sacks and stuck his foot in the doorway "—is a peace offering. Can I make you dinner?"

"What? And have you one-up me again?" Ali's hackles were well and truly raised.

"No." Aidan pressed his heels into the ground and made himself grow a couple of inches.

He knew he'd been a jerk, but he was hardly going to let Ali turn this situation into a free-for-all of notch-gathering. The North Stars' medical needs were ultimately his responsibility. And he knew the patients better than she did. *Fact.*

"I'm happy to have takeaway—or nothing, if you prefer—but we've got to sort this out."

"What, exactly?"

"You. Me. How we deal with things at work."

Ali rocked back in her woolly boots and he could almost see the decision-making process in her eyes.

"What were you going to make?"

"Risotto."

She pushed her lips out into a deep red moue and arched a brow.

"What kind?"

"Asparagus and lemon. My nan's recipe."

"I didn't know your nan was Italian."

"She wasn't—but I dare you to diss my nan's risotto."

"Ha!" Ali pulled open the door and let him pass. "Do you have her tucked around the corner somewhere?"

"Not tonight," Aidan mused as he carried the shopping to her kitchen island. "I wasn't certain if you'd offer to cook."

"That's something we both know is unlikely to happen." Ali padded over to him and began to nosy through the bags.

"You want to open up that wine I brought the other day?" He scanned the counter to see if it was still there. It was.

"You go ahead." Ali slipped onto one of the barstools and watched as Aidan began to hunt round her kitchen for knives or chopping boards or whatever it was he needed to make risotto. "I'm 'in between' drinks right now."

"Oh, yeah?" Aidan smiled up at her. "What does that mean?"

"It happens sometimes—I just can't pick what drink I like. Right now I'm leaning toward soda and lime."

"Jumping on the wagon?"

"No—" she started, then reconsidered. "Maybe. I don't know… Just haven't felt like drinking. It's my new boss." She pulled a face at him. "He's working me so hard I need to be at the top of my game so he'll stop *questioning my expert opinion* about things. Like injured clavicles near the pinch zone."

"Ali…"

"Yes?" She drummed her fingers along the kitchen island.

She was looking forward to an explanation. She was used to being in charge. Biting her tongue in front of her patients was not familiar terrain and she didn't like it. Not one bit.

"Here." Aidan handed her a knife and a big handful of asparagus. "Chop these up, will you?"

"Tell me why you undermined me today." She stood her ground. She wasn't going to be sidetracked and pushed into a sous chef role to boot.

"Honestly?" He looked at her and about a thousand thoughts jockeyed for pole position. "I'm…" he began, then reconsidered. "You're— This is all a big change. Having you here."

"Why? Because I'm a woman or because I'm

better at practicing medicine?" She gave him a sassy grin.

"Because you're different." Aidan responded tactically. "I know you would be hard-pressed to believe it—but I don't really do change. And having you here is one change after another, so you're going to have to be patient with me. I hired you because I respected your work. I'd like you to stay—but you're going to have to get used to working *with* me. We're meant to be a team. This isn't a one-woman chop shop, okay?"

Ali couldn't stop herself. She had to laugh. *One-woman chop shop?* That was a good one.

"Who doesn't like a bit of surgery?"

"*Me*! It's not my area of expertise and— Oh, for heaven's sake, Ali. Do I have to spell it out for you? I may be the CMO of one of Britain's best rugby squads and able to make a killer risotto, but *you* know your way around the surgery ward. It's impressive, Ali. Truly."

Their eyes met. He was *impressed* by her? Her lips twitched into a smile. She was tempted to do a little victory dance, but gloating wasn't her style.

"What was it you wanted me to do with this stuff?" She pointed at her cutting board.

"The asparagus? Small bite-sized pieces, please."

Ali began hacking away at the innocent asparagus stems and snuck a peek at Aidan, meticulously pithing a lemon. You did pith them, right? Something like that... With big strong hands attached to some rather lovely forearms...

He glanced across at her cutting board. "Easy there, Doctor. I hope you don't treat your patients like your asparagus."

"Sorry?" Talk about micromanaging! Hadn't they just been through this?

Aidan received the full force of her crackling blue eyes. "Don't glare at *me*! You're the one attacking it!" He couldn't help laughing at her furrowed brow. "Here—let me."

Aidan laid a hand on Ali's and gently guided her knife across the asparagus spears, slicing them into emerald green bite-sized pieces.

He felt her hand stiffen at his initial touch, but as they made their way through a few more of the fluid movements she began to relax. A warmth began to move from her hand to his, straight up his arm and across his shoulders. Being with her this way, doing something as familiar as cooking, was calming him. A welcome tonic after a hectic day with the North Stars. A heated memory of the night they'd shared. An unspoken suggestion of things to come.

He felt her hair brush against his cheek as she turned to face him. Her blue eyes were searching his. There was very little space between them and it would have been incredibly easy to just lean in and tease a few kisses out of her full lips. Lips he'd been aching to taste from the very moment they'd parted at the airport.

From the look on her face, she wouldn't stop him if he leaned in. He saw it in her eyes—just as he had the moment they had seen each other at the bar. Desire. Longing. But tonight it went deeper than that. If he touched her now he knew he wouldn't stop at a kiss, a simple caress. He couldn't. Not with her.

Ali reached him on a level he hadn't thought possible anymore. Not after the island, where his heart had gone numb with shock when he'd lost his grip on his childhood sweetheart's hand. He hadn't even begun to know how to mourn her.

How to honor her life—the future they would never have together. But from the very moment he had laid eyes on Ali he had felt *alive*. It was intoxicating, and he knew he was going to have to fight every cell in his body to maintain control.

Abruptly, Aidan returned to the other side of the kitchen island. He—they—had made a deal. A professional relationship. That was all he and Ali would share. He didn't look at her, but he could tell Ali felt it, too. The connection. The silent *simpatico* he couldn't quite define. It was a heated medley of disappointment, understanding, expectation and stasis. This close, he could smell her perfume—something a little citrusy? A bit of clean linen? It suited her. As did the blue top she wore. It made her sea-blue eyes that much harder to resist.

Aidan felt his controlled exterior weaken.

He glanced over at Ali, who was now sawing away at some cherry tomatoes for the salad.

"Is this another example of your technique in the operating theater?"

Ali bristled. What did he know about her? Her work? What did he know about *anything*?

One minute he was doing a sexy kitchen version of *Ghost* with her, making pulses of heat strobe throughout her body, and the next he was making narky comments about the one thing in the world she knew she excelled at.

"You know where the door is, Dr. Tate." She couldn't keep an edge from her voice. "No one's forcing you to stay."

"Easy there, pet. I was just teasing."

As quickly as he'd irked her, his gentle voice calmed her down. Aidan's Northern accent wasn't strong, but this was the first time the regional term of endearment she'd been hearing all week had made her knees turn to jelly. Good thing she was parked on a stool.

Come to think of it, no one had had that effect on her. *Ever.* Sure, she'd had boyfriends—if you could call someone you'd dated for a few months a boyfriend. Her work had always been her go-to partner. Never before had she met someone who came close to being both. Not that Aidan was. He was her colleague. Her boss. "The Suit" was someone she wouldn't meet again.

Ali squeezed her eyes tight, listening as Aidan stirred rice into a pan of frying shallots. He poured in some liquid that immediately released a heady, steamy, intoxicating scent. It smelled the way she felt when Aidan looked at her. A bit other-worldly.

She sighed, rubbing her fingers across her eyes. She didn't know if she could stand another hour of ping-ponging emotions, let alone three months of working together.

"Look." She put the knife down on the cutting board filled with asparagus and tomatoes. "Cooking is clearly not my arena. It's yours. I'll do what I'm good at and select some music."

"Is that a challenge?"

"No, it's not," she snapped. Did *everything* have to be a competition? "I just know my area of expertise is not anywhere around *this* part of the apartment." She waved her arms around the open-plan kitchen area.

"Being around the players all day must bring out the combatant in me." Aidan held his hands up in the surrender position, one hand clothed in a flowery oven mitt, the other holding a pink-handled spatula. Another internet purchase.

Ali looked at him standing there, this absolute picture of manhood, bedecked with flowery kitchen gear, and couldn't help bursting out laughing.

Aidan feigned surprise that she should find his appearance funny, and then joined in her laughter. It felt good. Relaxing.

"Truce?" He offered her the hand with the oven mitt on it.

Still giggling, Ali took the oven mitt and shook it with a somber expression.

"Truce. Not that I know what we were fighting about, but a truce sounds perfect. I need a mate up here."

Aidan's eyes widened.

"A friend—a *friend*!" Ali covered, quickly busying herself with her music collection. *Nice one, Ali.* That's some top Freudian slippage, right there.

Aidan's expression turned serious as he returned to the risotto, giving it an occasional stir, visibly trying to formulate what he was going to say next.

"Ali, I want you to know I'm glad you're here. That you're part of the team."

She held her breath, a little nervous that there was a *however* attached to this kind statement.

Aidan poured in another dollop of stock, waited for the sizzle and whoosh of steam then looked up at her. He took a thoughtful sip of wine, swished it around a bit and then swallowed. He reminded Ali of one of those annoying wine critics on TV.

"Your CV is flawless and the team couldn't ask for anyone better. Apart from—"

"Apart from...?" Ali tried to tease the rest of his sentence out of him without exploding in fury.

"Me, of course." And then he released another one of those perfectly gorgeous smiles.

Unable to help herself, Ali fell apart with an enormous belly laugh. You didn't get as good as this man was rumored to be without a healthy splash of arrogance.

She raised an invisible glass to him, "Touché, Dr. Tate. Touché."

"Let's put that asparagus in, then. We need to get some food into you—then it's straight to bed. Tomorrow's another big day."

Ali felt heat creep into her cheeks for the second time that night and hid her face in her hands.

It was all too easy to imagine Aidan carrying her into her sparsely decorated bedroom and having his manly way with her. *Again.*

She peered at Aidan through her fingers. She had come up here to shake things up a bit, and there was no contesting the fact that meeting him again had done that to a tee!

"Asparagus, please, chef."

Aidan's voice broke into her thoughts, sending another disconcerting tangle of heat twirling round her stomach.

"It's tender enough that it can just steam in amongst the rice."

She slid the cutting board across the island and watched as he fluidly cascaded the delicate spears into the creamy risotto. He gave the mixture a few swift turns, then pulled a couple of plates out of the oven.

She raised an eyebrow.

"You didn't expect your risotto on a *cold* plate, did you?"

*From you it's hard to know what to expect.*

Aidan joined Ali on the spare stool at the kitchen bar as her dining room chairs were nonexistent.

They ate heartily and silently.

Aidan frowned at his risotto. Not because it wasn't good. It was excellent and he knew it. He was confused as to why Ali was living like a Buddhist monk.

"So, is this what you Southerners call 'Extreme Living'?" He tried to keep his voice light, but saw that his comment had chafed. Her eyes had clouded over with something he couldn't quite put a finger on. Loneliness? Sorrow?

That was it. Sorrow.

*Nice one, Aidan.* Seemed he just couldn't keep his foot out of his mouth tonight.

"Call it what you please, but I like it this way."

Her tone was curt and there was defiance in her expression, daring him to suggest that her home should be otherwise.

"I think it suits you."

"What's *that* supposed to mean?"

He could see she didn't know whether to smile or be insulted. "It looks like the home of someone who has something to hide."

A flash of anger crossed her face.

"Why would you think I have something to hide?"

He took another mouthful of rice, pretty certain he wasn't meant to answer. Her lips parted as she took in a deep breath, then began speaking again, using her fork to visibly accent her key points.

"So I wanted to try something new! What's so bad about that?" She raised an attitude-filled eyebrow at him—if such a thing was possible.

"Not a thing."

"Damn tootin' right! I suppose *your* flat is stuffed to the gills with furniture? Or is it more magazine-spread-ready, in case you're chosen to be the centerfold for *Physio Monthly*?"

Ali smiled broadly as that picture fleshed itself out in her mind. *Uh-oh. Wait a minute.* He was naked in her mental picture. Not so very professional. She looked over at Aidan—*fully clothed* Aidan—to see if she could shake the image from her head.

The only things in her line of vision were his perfect lips. There was a bit of a five o'clock shadow in her sightline—the kind that made him appear just the opposite of scruffy.

Rugged. Male. Kissable.

If she thought she'd had butterflies before, her stomach went into full flip-flop overdrive mode now, when he reached for her hand, as if to say, *It's okay. I'm not attacking you.*

Ali nearly fell backward off the stool as her mobile phone began a little dance on the counter, the vibration and ringtone breaking through the thick atmosphere.

"Sorry," she mumbled, abruptly pulling her hand away from his.

Grabbing her phone, she walked to the far end of the large loft.

"Hello?" Ali knew her voice sounded unnaturally high, and she forced a slow breath between her lips to try to steady herself.

She held the telephone close to her ear, willing it to stop the roar of blood racing through her entire system. She could feel Aidan's eyes on her, but she refused to turn around, focusing instead on the twinkling lights of the city reflected in the wide river steadily flowing past. She wished her nerves were a tenth as calm.

"Doc? It's Rory."

"Hi, Rory. How's the collarbone? Is everything all right?"

Ali struggled to control her breath. She was really going to have to get a grip. Three more months of "friendship" with Aidan Tate was going to be much harder than she thought. She knew how moody and defensive she was coming across to him, but for some reason he brought out the extremes of all her emotions!

"Not really."

Ali's emotions sobered quickly, her years of medical training coming to the fore.

"You're not feeling light-headed, are you? Finding it hard to breathe?"

"No, Doc. Nothing like that." She heard him inhale sharply before continuing in a tight voice, "It's just that I was practicing with the resistance bands and—"

*"What?"* Ali felt her eyebrows fly up and couldn't help raising her voice. "You were meant to be resting it tonight. Icing it!"

"Yeah, I know." She heard the remorse in Rory's voice as he continued, "I thought I'd get a head start on rehab, so I'd be ready for the match, but I think I've made it worse."

"Rory, I need you to lie down on the floor if you're not already. I'm going to call an ambulance."

"Don't be ridiculous."

Before she could continue with Rory, she felt the phone being taken from her hand.

Blood rushed to her face. How *dared* he? She was consulting with her patient. Aidan had already undermined her once today—and now he had the cheek to grab her phone from her in her own home?

Wheeling around to retrieve the phone, she saw Aidan holding out an arm as if to keep her at bay.

Unbelievable. He was so insecure he couldn't even let her speak to one of "their" patients. *This was going to have to stop.*

"Rory—it's Aidan here. Are you able to get to the clinic, mate?" He paused, looking intently into Ali's eyes.

She felt her cheeks burn, ashamed that the heat came from a mix of frustration and attraction. The whole situation was ridiculous. She leaned her head against the cool window to try to regain some levity. If this was how the next few months were going to be, it was never going to work. She was too advanced in her career to be treated like a junior doctor.

Taking a deep breath, Ali reached out and took back her phone. "Rory, it's Dr. Lockhart again. I'm going to put you on speaker so we can get you the best treatment straight away, all right?"

This time she kept her gaze steady, noting Aidan's eyebrows rising a fraction, while the rest of his face remained neutral.

"Hi, Docs." Rory couldn't keep the confusion as to why they were together out of his voice, "I'm not sure, exactly, but when I was working with the resistance bands I think I dislodged my clavicle, and it seems to be in a weirder place than it was before."

Ali glanced over to Aidan. Reading those darkening eyes of his was virtually impossible.

Pulling her eyes away, she continued. "Rory, you could've just dislocated it again, and I can fix that pretty quickly, but from what you're saying there's a chance the fracture has become compounded. The bone could move and pinch your carotid artery. We definitely don't want *that* to happen. Are you alone?"

"Uh...not exactly."

"Mate." Aidan redirected his gaze to the phone, "Ali is right. You need to get on the floor immediately and have your guest get some ice, or frozen peas—whatever you have in the house—on that shoulder now. We'll be over as soon as possible. Got it?"

"Sure, Doc," Rory's voice was sounding a bit weaker now.

"Hang in there, Rory. We won't be long. If you begin to feel short of breath, or if any extremely sharp pains run down your arm, have your—erm—*friend* call an ambulance immediately."

Ali ended the call and started scrolling through her address book for Rory's details. She'd entered all of the players' numbers and addresses into her mobile phone the previous week, just in case anything like this happened. She just hadn't expected "anything" to pop up so quickly.

"I'll drive." Aidan's voice sounded commanding. *Surprise, surprise.*

"Look, Dr. Tate—"

"Oh, we're back to formal titles now, are we?" Aidan taunted as he strode across her apartment to the door, not even bothering to look at her as he spoke.

Wow. This man really knew how to rankle. The *arrogance*!

"Yes. This is a professional situation and I'm not going to spend the next few months begging you for permission to treat a patient. I don't think I need to remind you who it was he rang."

Ali kept her voice steady, but knew if she let go of the kitchen counter she was clenching her knees might betray the wobble they felt.

"And I don't think I need to remind *you* who knows their way around the city."

"Fine. You drive. But when we get there—he's my patient." Ali's eyes sparked brightly as she spoke.

Aidan noted with a sense of admiration that she had managed to keep her voice level, even though he was pretty certain she was fuming. Truth be told, if someone had treated *him* as he'd just treated her...for a second time... Well, it wouldn't have been pretty.

"Meet you in the garage in five?"

"Fine."

Aidan took the stairs to his own apartment. How had he managed to make such a hash of their new "working relationship" so quickly?

He slipped the key into his door.

Simple. Rory had called Ali and not him. It rankled. He had always been the go-to man for the team. The only consistent medic in their lives. Despite having to be available round the clock, and forsaking what little social life he had, he had enjoyed having the team's trust. He'd been their medical point man. And now, in just one short fortnight Ali had become their first port of call.

His mind raced with the things he could've done wrong with Rory. Had he set the figure-eight brace incorrectly this afternoon? He'd followed the usual checklist, hadn't he? Or had he been too concerned with getting back out on the field and asserting his control over Ali?

Aidan shook his head clear, knowing he was going to have to face some hard truths. And soon. He kept trying to control her because she brought out a side in him he'd thought was long gone.

A few strides into his loft and a quick look to the right revealed that his medical bag was where he always left it—in the unused contemporary fireplace. Medicine. That was what got him charged. Sent fire through his veins.

Romantic evenings by the fireside weren't really his thing.

Perhaps it was time to reconsider. He didn't like the way he was treating this perfectly innocent woman who'd appeared in his life, rattled his cage and given him a good old-fashioned dose of

reality. But romantic evenings by the fireside...?
Not really appropriate.

He wondered if she'd ever been to kickboxing...

He grabbed his bag and shut the door behind
him. *Work*. That was what he needed to focus
on. Not one hundred and one ways to spend time
with Ali Lockhart. She was his colleague and
that was it.

# CHAPTER FOUR

A TWENTYSOMETHING BLONDE woman pulled open the front door to Rory's palatial modern house when they arrived before shrinking into the corner of the well-appointed room, from where she silently watched as Ali and Aidan knelt on either side of the player.

The moment Ali saw Rory's ashen face she knew he'd done more than dislocate his collarbone joint. A separated shoulder wouldn't tent like this. He'd compounded the fracture.

"Pulse is up. Too high." Aidan's voice was professional, efficient, as he took the player's obs.

"Rory, don't try to move. Are you able to follow my finger with your eyes?" Ali raised her index finger a few inches above Rory's pale face and watched as he tried to follow her moving it slowly in an arc. His breath started to come in short, sharp bursts.

"Shuuurrre, Doc..." Rory's speech was barely audible, and decidedly slurred.

"I think he's compounded the clavicle and pinched the carotid. He'll need surgery."

"You're sure?"

"As sure as I can be without an X-ray, but we don't have that luxury." Ali was relieved to hear that Aidan's question hadn't been laced with doubt. It had been just one professional confirming a course of action with another. "Call an ambulance. He'll need to get this plated and he shouldn't be moved without a proper stretcher."

"On it."

Ali's energies were entirely on Rory. If his carotid artery was pinched for much longer it could lead to a stroke, changing the young man's life forever. Time was of the essence.

"This isn't going to feel good, Rory. I need you to try your best to focus, all right?"

Glancing up at the young woman in the corner, Ali motioned toward a cushion on the long white leather sofa.

"Could you bring that cushion over for him?" The girl didn't move. "It's all right," Ali reassured her, "This will help him."

Two quick strides and Aidan was at Rory's side, cushion in hand, phone cradled between his shoulder and ear, holding on to the player's hand.

"As big a breath as you can muster, mate—ready?"

Aidan looked up at Ali and gave her a quick nod of assent. Time was against them and she needed to act now.

Placing her hands on Rory's neck and clavicle, Ali deftly felt for what was surely a compound fracture and realigned the bones as quickly and adroitly as she could.

Rory howled in pain and there was a rush of blood to his face. A welcome sight after the ghostly pallor he had worn when they'd first arrived.

"Hold him—he needs to stay stationary. This relocation isn't permanent."

Aidan responded quickly, placing a knee on the player's good shoulder as Ali pressed down the best she could on his injured side with the melting packet of frozen peas and what looked to be a sirloin steak she'd found lying by Rory's side.

She looked up again at the woman in the corner and gave her a reassuring smile. "You did well to keep him flat and have his shoulder iced. What's your name?"

"Amber."

Her voice was so soft Ali strained to hear her. She seemed nice.

"Amber. That's a lovely name." She offered her another smile and then tipped her head in the direction she assumed was the kitchen. "Would you be able to get together a bag or a tea towel filled with as much ice as you can find?

Looking back at Rory, who had his eyes clenched tight with pain but was breathing more regularly, Ali kept her voice low and steady.

"Rory? You've bashed yourself up a bit more than we thought, so we're going to have to go to hospital, all right?" His eyes fluttered open in acknowledgment. "We're most likely going to put a plate on your clavicle, which will give you a sexy little scar, but hopefully it will get you playing for the final."

Rory smiled and made a move as if to sit up.

"Oh, no, you don't!" Aidan removed his knee from the player's shoulder and quickly pressed down on it with one of his hands.

"Stay down, Ror— Ali's got you covered on this one."

Ali looked up, sensing Aidan's eyes upon her. She caught her breath as their eyes met. Felt her teeth bite into her lower lip. He hadn't deemed her capable of taking a phone call half an hour ago, but now he was happy to let her take the proverbial driver's seat and bring Rory into surgery. Would wonders never cease?

"Do you know who's on the surgical staff at Tealside?"

"Why? You're not up to it?"

Ali thinned her eyes, to assess if he was taunting her. His look was open, curious. It was not an attempt to catch her out. It was just a question.

Releasing Rory's shoulder, she gave herself a mental shake. She was going to have to stop being so distrustful. Keeping Aidan at arm's length was only going to be tough if she made it that way. She took a deep breath and decided to go with trust. It was the only way this "relationship" was going to work.

"I just thought we'd better see who was on at the hospital to make sure I don't push any noses out of joint. If they've got a shoulder specialist they'd be better placed to do the op. But I'm happy to do it if no one else is available."

"I'm not sure, but the paramedics can find out en route. They should be here any minute."

Aidan was impressed that Ali knew where to start and stop with her levels of treatment. It was clear her patient's health was paramount. Other surgeons liked the glory. Who *wouldn't* want to add award-winning North Stars player Rory Stiles to their tick-list of surgeries? Particularly when his place on the team could mean a win or lose in the final.

A thick lock of shimmering black hair had come loose from her ponytail and now hung across her right eye. He had to fight the distinctly unprofessional urge to reach up and brush it behind her ear. Just slip it back into place before running his finger along her jawline. Just like every colleague did for another. *Not!*

"Well, I'd prefer it if you do the surgery." His voice was huskier than he'd hoped, but he continued anyway. "It'll be better in the long run as you'll know exactly what to do for follow-up. Let's get him stabilized at the hospital and hope you can put the plate in tomorrow."

"We should probably see what the preliminary X-rays show. The last thing Rory needs is inflammation pressuring the carotid."

"Absolutely—let's check everything. But regardless of who's on staff at Tealside, I think you're the best man—*woman*—for the job."

"You're positive you'd be happy for me to run with this?"

"He's sure!" Rory croaked up at them, cracking a crooked smile. "And would you two stop flirting over me? It reminds me of the night I'm *not* going to be having with Amber."

Aidan resisted an urge to punch Rory in the arm. They hadn't been flirting. They'd been speaking professionally. Cordially. Respectfully. Like workmates.

He chanced a glance at Ali, whose cheeks had flushed crimson and who was busily chewing on her exquisite apple-red lips. She didn't look happy.

*Fine. Hands up!* He'd been flirting.

In a professional manner.

It was about as close to flirting as he got, and Rory—the team's king of leaving broken hearts in his wake—ought to know.

It seemed everyone in the room was holding

their breath. Could the tension in the room get any higher?

Aidan felt a sigh of relief escape his lips as Amber ran into the room, lugging a pillowcase filled nearly to the brim with ice cubes.

"I found an ice machine in the games room. Is this enough?"

If ever there was a time to be grateful to ride in the back of an ambulance it was now. Ali kept her hand on Rory's shoulder as a paramedic took his obs and gave him a couple of milligrams of painkiller. She'd asked him not to dose him up to the hilt before they knew what procedures they would need to carry out tonight.

An unfortunate side effect of feeling better was that Rory had got chatty. *Real* chatty.

"Yeah, he's definitely into you, Harty."

"Who?" She could play dumb for a bit, right?

"Tate! I've never seen him so weird. Man, earlier on the field I thought he was going to have a fit!"

Ali stiffened. "Because a woman was treating you?"

"No, Doc. You got it all wrong." Rory waved

for her to come closer, even though he didn't lower the decibel level of his voice an iota. "He *fancies* you."

"Don't be daft!" She swatted at him, feeling not a little mortified that the paramedic was quite merrily enjoying their conversation.

"You know," Rory continued, clearly enjoying the topic, "you could always take on The Monk as a special project..."

"The Monk? And that is..." She chanced a glance over at the paramedic, who was feigning deafness. It must make the earwigging easier.

"Dr. *Taaaaaaaate*..." Rory drawled, the meds taking him swinging toward Sleepyville.

The Monk, huh? Interesting... She had pegged Aidan for one of those "girl at every away game" types. With looks like his and that bobby-dazzler of a smile... Hmm... Maybe being judgmental didn't suit her either.

"We've been trying to set him up for *aaaaages*. Never takes, though."

"Never takes what?"

Rory's lids began a losing war to stay open.

*For heaven's sake. Don't fall asleep on me now!*

Ali pressed her hands to the bench of the ambulance to steady herself as it slowed and turned into what must be the hospital forecourt.

Her mind flicked back into work mode. Exactly where it should have been for the ten-minute ride. She'd need to get X-rays, make some quick decisions about how quickly Rory did or didn't need surgery, and then try to grab some sleep if she was going to be in theater in a few hours' time.

The ambulance pulled to a stop and the back doors virtually burst open to reveal none other than a grinning Aidan Tate.

"Hey, look! It's Beauty and the Beast!"

Ali's jaw dropped open, then clapped shut as Rory gave her a heavy-lidded *I told you so* wink.

Aidan gave Ali a sidelong glance. The X-rays were looking the opposite of good. She'd been right all along. A preventative op would have prevented the fracture compound and the carotid arterial pinch. It might easily have been fatal. In practice, he preferred to steer clear of surgery unless it was necessary, but in this case he should've known Rory would push the boundaries. This year's final meant the world to the team.

Ali's profile was giving nothing away. Nor was

she. She had been tight-lipped since their arrival at the hospital.

"Fancy a coffee?"

"I think some sleep might be in order." Ali continued to frown at the X-rays, then asked, "What time did you say the theater is booked?

"Six a.m."

They both glanced at the clock hanging above the X-ray light board. Just gone midnight.

"Right. I'd better head home. Is there a taxi rank anywhere?"

She looked around the room as if it might offer her an answer. Anywhere but at him. What had he done now?

"Oh, didn't I say?"

Ali looked at him blankly.

"I took the liberty of organizing one of the on-call surgeons' rooms for you here. Unless the idea of a resident's room makes you run for the hills?"

"No, that sounds fine." Her expression was inscrutable. "I'm not fussy. So long as they've got a toothbrush and some scrubs I could borrow."

"Great. I've already popped some things in there for us."

*"Us?"* Her tone spoke volumes. The not-a-chance-in-hell variety.

"Yes. Us. I was hoping to watch the master at work." He crossed his heart and gave her a silly grin. "I'm not being a control freak, if that's what you're worried about—honest!"

She quirked an eyebrow, unconvinced. He had to admit the idea of spending a night in such close proximity to Ali had set off blaring sirens, warning that staying in the Pal Zone would be tough. He mentally crossed his fingers.

"I'll be on my best behavior. Scout's Honor."

"Well..." She eyed him suspiciously, arms firmly crossed. "How high did you get in the Scouts?"

"Explorer." Actually, he'd been a nerd, and had stayed on as part of the Scout Network for a long time, but she didn't need to know that.

"That's *it*? My cousin made it to Scout Network, and he was a city boy. No deal."

"Fine—you got me. I stayed on until I started med school. Three years of Scout Network. You can trust me." He made the Scout's Honor sign again for good measure.

"Dr. Tate?" Ali's lips began to shift into a grin.

"Were you trying to look *cool* by saying you stopped at Explorer?"

"Maybe." He returned the grin, then pointed toward the wall clock. "T-minus six hours, Doctor. It's time to start counting sheep."

Aidan swung his arm in a dramatic *This way, madam*, gesture and felt his lips thin as she passed him. Staying in his own bunk when all the others had been filled with scouts was easy. Doing the same with Ali not a meter above him…?

Maybe the visitor's chair in Rory's room would be a better choice.

"And we're ready to close."

Ali stepped back from the surgical table, grateful that it had been a straightforward op. The plate and screw fixation were in, and would hopefully allow for early mobilization. If Rory had listened to them he would've been looking at four to six weeks' recovery for the fracture—now he was looking at closer to three months, but with a better guarantee of proper bone union.

The big North v South match was barely beyond the three-month marker. When he was up for it she was going to give him one meaty lecture. As the surgical team moved in to close she glanced over at the observation room, where Aidan was giving her a quick thumbs-up and a grin.

Despite her best intentions to totally block him out, she felt like warm sunbeams were shooting out from her chest. Good grief! Since when did she need a thumbs-up approval rating on a simple plate-and-screw surgery?

"Do you think Dr. Tate's going to wait for Rory in Recovery?" a nurse asked quietly.

"You'll have to ask him yourself. I'm not his keeper."

Ali hoped her words hadn't sounded as sharp as they had in her head. Keeping tabs on Aidan was most definitely not on her "to-do" list. Especially now, after she'd gone into the bunkroom he'd booked for them and then he had never shown up. Not that sleeping would've come easily if he *had* been in the same room. But even so she had felt the loss of not being with him.

Getting up for surgery had been the only way to clear herself of the growing realization that Aidan Tate was making an impact on her. A big one.

Surgery was the one zone where she was able

to shut everything else out—thank God. But one thumbs-up and a rakish smile later here she was, back in the land of reminding her knees that the rest of her body would like to remain upright.

"Sorry," the nurse continued. "It's just that he's never stayed with a patient overnight before, so I assumed…"

The poor woman's voice petered out as Ali's eyes widened. Then the nurse carried on, as if Ali had told her talking about Aidan was her absolute favorite thing in the whole wide world. Maybe it was. Was it…?

"For a little while we all thought he was going to stay in the surgeon's bunk with *you*!"

"Oh?" Ali replied non-committally.

"Don't worry!" The nurse laughed. "We've all tried to break the impenetrable veneer of 'The Monk.' No one's managed. Keeps himself to himself. But he's about as dishy as they come, don't you think?"

Ali kept her eyes on the vacant spot in the observation room where he had been. *Yes. Yes, she did think.* Not that she was going to tell the nurse. "I hadn't really noticed. He's all yours!"

Ali left the theater quickly, heading back to

the locker room where she'd hung her clothes. She needed to change, check on Rory in Recovery and then get back to Aidan. *No!* That wasn't right. Get back to work. *Work.* Where she was learning new things. From Aidan. Like finding out that she could reach a ridiculously divine orgasm when he did those soft kisses and silky-smooth caresses all along her—

"Lockhart?"

*Speak of the devil.*

"Coming!" Ali tugged her jumper down, grabbed her bag and careened out the door, narrowly avoiding colliding into one very familiar chest.

Aidan steadied her, his brown eyes seeking an explanation for her frenetic behavior. She shrugged herself out of his hold and headed for Recovery. Minimal contact meant minimal heat detonations in her erogenous zones, right?

"Lockhart...?"

She stopped and gave Aidan a pointed look. He was interrupting her No Touching pep talk to herself.

"You all right?" He leaned against the doorframe in that really annoying I'm-a-deeply-sexy-supermodel way. "Want to come to the gym with me later? You look like you've got some energy to burn."

A flash of white teeth and a wink followed the statement.

Ali looked Aiden straight in the eye and blew a steadying breath between her lips. Gym buddy or not—he was asking for it. Her fingers were curled into tight fists and she could feel adrenaline begin to charge her. Four weeks into her time Up North and she'd managed to avoid this sort of confrontation with Aidan, but here they were, face-to-face, and she was on the attack.

*You can do this. Piece of cake.* She wriggled her fingers into new fists and did a couple of quick hops back and forth. *You will do this.* She would be ready to go in just…three, two, one— and in an explosive shift of her weight she began to kick as if her life depended on it.

"Is that it?" Aidan grinned back at her, completely unfazed by her power moves. "That's all you're good for? C'mon. You're worse than last week. Give it to me, Harty. Harder."

He wanted hard? She could do hard. Ali shifted

her weight again and gave the punching bag all she had.

Aidan barely blinked. "C'mon, Lockhart! You call those stitches on Mack's forehead today *butterfly*? Dr. Frankenstein could have done a better job!"

"Oh, you want to play dirty, do you?" *Bam!* She gave the punching bag a satisfying whack.

"A double specialty in physio and orthopedic surgery? Peanuts. A chimpanzee could've topped that."

*Bash!*

"And I had to rewrap Jonesey's wrist today—twice!"

*Biff!* That was a lie and he knew it. This was getting to be fun!

"You kiss like a girl."

*What?*

She hadn't really heard him above the blare of the music. Was he dissing her kissing? Ali went still, leveled her gaze at him and shook her head slowly.

Now that was *low*. They'd both been very diligent about avoiding any mention of "That Night..." But if that was how he wanted to play it—

"I kiss like a *woman*." The depth of her assertion surprised even herself. She watched Aidan's eyes widen as hers narrowed. She twisted her body into an almighty whirling dervish spin and kicked the bag with all her might. *"Don't mock my kissing!"*

Ali was flat on her back before she could say *boo*. The rest of the kickboxing class fell silent, the air thick with the thump-pump of dance tracks blaring out from the speakers.

Had she said *kissing*? Aidan dropped to Ali's side, horrified. Her footing must have gone wrong in the kick and she'd ended up flat on her back. Everything slipped into a horror-film-style slow motion. *This was his fault.* He had pushed her. Just like he'd pushed his girlfriend to go snorkeling all those years ago. *Try new things! Reach for new limits!* What the hell was wrong with him?

Someone turned off the music and flicked on the overhead lights. Ali was out cold.

*This isn't happening...this isn't happening!*

His mouth went dry as he tried to gather his wits. No blood pooling at the back of her head. Good. He felt along her neck and the back of her head for any obvious injuries. Ali's pure blue eyes remained firmly shut.

He cupped her face in his hands, frantically repeating her name again and again, his thumb caressing her forehead, her cheek. He'd totally been lying when he'd told her she meant nothing to him. He'd come to rely on her these past few weeks. More than that. He couldn't get enough of her. Every minute of every day he wanted to be with Ali and find out more. More about what made her tick. More about what she liked...didn't like.

All of his medical skills seemed to abandon him. He was a *doctor*, for God's sake. Shouldn't he be checking her eyes? Her obs? Doing something medical?

This sort of injury happened in team practice and in games often enough—a person being knocked to the ground so hard the brain's electrical patterns were disrupted—and they always treated head injuries with intense scrutiny. The ramifications of a bad blow were huge. There could be a rupture to the brain's membrane or to the brain tissue, which could lead to arterial damage, which in turn could lead to brain damage or a fatal blood clot.

*She could die.*

Aidan lifted his eyes up to the ceiling as if it would give him some answers. *What had he done?* Critically injured the one person who was beginning to make him feel alive again?

"Aidan?"

Ali's voice was a low croak, her eyes slowly working their way open, making an immediate connection with his own. There had never been a pair of eyes he was more happy to see.

"Ali! Can you hear me? Don't move your head."

He didn't care if she saw the gloss of tears in his eyes. She was okay! Maybe he would tell her how his feelings were changing. How spending time with her made him feel like being a whole person again. A whole person who felt every single minute of the past few weeks had been supercharged with vitality...life.

"Follow my finger. Just follow the arc of my finger."

Ali's eyes didn't move. They stayed locked with his. A wash of emotion sent his heart lurching into his throat.

"You're right," Ali whispered.

"About what?" Aidan ran his fingers through her hair—he couldn't help it. Every pore in his body wanted to look after this woman, to care for each intensely passionate, über-talented and deeply sexy cell of her.

"My kicking could do with some improvement!" Ali flashed him a cheeky grin and popped up from the floor, her hands already in sparring position, feet hopping back and forth. *Float like a butterfly...sting like an Ali.*

"Alexis Lockhart! Were you *faking* being knocked out?"

Another broad smile met his indignant question.

"You're lucky I don't pop you one in the kisser."

He pushed himself up from the floor, his chest burning with a whole new mix of feelings. Indignation was winning the battle, but she had properly frightened him. And made him realize something very clearly. *He cared.* He cared about Alexis Lockhart. This was much more than a professional relationship to him. That didn't sit well. Not one teeny, tiny speck.

"C'mon, Tate." Ali jiggled her head from side

to side, oblivious to the turmoil she'd created in his heart. "What did you expect? You've been doing this for years and I've been doing it for a few weeks. I've got to work with my assets, and tonight I aced psyching you *right* out of the park! *Ha!* You should see yourself. You're white as a ghost!"

"And your point is…?" Aidan knew hands on hips wasn't his best look, but he had to restrain himself from shaking her—or, more to the point, from pulling her into his arms and telling her never to do such a stupid thing again.

He'd been nanoseconds away from smothering her in kisses and sweet nothings when she'd opened her eyes. Heaven had been merciful and saved him that embarrassment. These were playground tricks. He should've seen it coming a mile away—particularly having witnessed how easily she could spar verbally with the lads. He couldn't *believe* he'd been on the brink of telling her he *cared*. Lucky break.

"No point—just saying. A girl's gotta do…" Ali stopped herself, suddenly very aware that there was a lot more going on in Aidan's eyes than superficial concern. Her prank had really shaken him.

What was *that* all about? She'd thought their whole joshing, jokey mates thing had been working pretty well in terms of keeping the sexual tension at bay. At the very least it had meant they could spend more time together without constantly being under threat of being arrested by the kissing police. Maybe she'd pushed too hard. It didn't feel right to know she'd hurt him.

"Let's say we even out the playing field, seeing as you're obviously the kickboxing master." Ali began unraveling the tape he'd strapped her into at the beginning of class. "I've done your kickboxing malarkey for quite a few weeks now. I think it's time you did something *I'm* good at." She sized him up, hoping her heavy-lidded, high-browed gaze would make him a bit nervous.

Nope. Steady as they came. The "Great Wall of Tate" face.

It was time to pull out the big guns. "Let's just see if you're up to matching a bit of girl power."

"And that would be what, exactly?" He crossed his arms, visibly dubious that she could come up with anything that would get her one up on him.

"Apart from dance injury medicine, which I already know you stink at?" She didn't really—but they were still sparring. Just a little…

"And cooking, which we know *you* stink at?" Aidan added, beginning to enjoy their tête-à-tête.

She spread her hands out in front of him as if presenting him with a sign. "Ninety continuous minutes of hot yoga."

The smug expression immediately dropped from his face. "Hot what?"

"You heard me. You wouldn't be afraid of leaving your comfort zone, would you? Hot yoga. You and me." She made the *I see you* gesture with her fingers. "After practice tomorrow. No more of this namby-pamby kickboxery."

She spun toward the door with a small sniff, rubbed the back of her head—which she *had* actually conked a bit—and flounced away the best she could in her trainers and sweat-soaked gym gear. *Hot yoga. That'll separate the boys from the men.*

Ten minutes later, in the privacy of the men's locker room shower, Aidan let the shakes he knew he needed to purge begin. He pressed his hands against the tile wall and let the water stream down his head and back. Seeing Ali lying on the floor like that had been a knife in the heart. Nothing short of pure bravura had helped him keep up their light-hearted banter.

He'd never even had the chance to see Mary's body. Nor had he had a chance to propose. Sensible as ever, he'd wanted to wait until toward the end of their holiday, to make sure they got on in every type of scenario. They'd made it through school, then uni—separate ones, she'd wanted to teach—and she'd waited patiently for him when he'd gone off to medical school. She had been his steady-as-they-came girl. The ring and her body had both been washed away, along with God knew what or who else, when the storm had struck.

Aidan lifted his face up into the stream of water, willing the shower to flush away the sting of tears teasing at his nostrils. This was the closest he'd come to crying about that day, and he didn't know if he could handle opening that particular door. It had been well over five years ago, but the shock he'd felt at seeing Ali lying there today had brought it all back to the fore. He couldn't lose another person—not one that he cared about.

He pulled his head out of the steaming water, blinked away the droplets and looked around the stall, as if the tiles might start explaining the situation to him.

Was this real? Was he really beginning to care about Ali? Had their being together developed into something deeper than the raw attraction he knew they felt for one another?

His body reminded him of their physical connection every time he saw her afresh. There was no getting away from that. But they had sensibly and proactively reshaped the sexy tension between them into the perfect cocktail of—in turn—ignoring each other, taking jabs at one another's medical practices and spending just about every waking minute they had together. As if it were a means of constant checking that the other person wasn't going back on their deal to keep things professional.

They hadn't so much as shared a goodnight kiss. It was hardly as if he was falling in love with her.

His breath caught in his throat.

*Was* he?

*Nah.* She was a good-time girl. Of course he respected her professionally, but it was easy enough to see that the girl didn't do long-term anything. Just like him. A perfect match.

Aidan blew a raspberry into the stream of water and loaded his hand with a good-sized squirt of shower gel. She'd just given him a bit of a fright. Served him right for pushing her so hard.

Hot yoga, eh? *Bring it on, Lockhart!*

# CHAPTER FIVE

AIDAN WASN'T ENTIRELY sure he'd be able to un-
fold his legs out of the pretzel shape he'd somehow cajoled them into. Ali hadn't been kidding
when she'd said ninety minutes of hot yoga would
be a challenge. Walking out upright would be a
feat at this juncture. And she had upped the po-
tential for humiliation stakes by inviting as many
lads from the team as she could. *Cross-training,
my eye!*

He looked round at the players who'd agreed to
come along and saw similar expressions of con-
sternation on their faces. It was impossible to
stop a smile from forming when his eyes landed
on her. There in the center of the class, looking
as Buddha-calm as could be, her legs folded into
a perfect lotus position, rail-straight spine and
gently bowed head, was his ebony-haired colleague.

The class might have been meant to center him,

but ever since Ali had arrived in his life he felt as if the earth's surface had shifted into a wobble board. She was shaking some cast-in-stone positions he'd held. Like not mixing business and pleasure, for one. And that was a *big* one.

"You still lining things up with your chi, there, Tatey?"

Aidan looked up at Mack—one of the players—who was offering him a hand to get up. He grabbed it gratefully.

"Or were you in the Lockhart Zone?"

"What?" Aidan dropped the young player's hand as if it was a burning coal, making a quick check to see if anyone had been listening.

"Tate, you transparent slice of manhood!" Mack's eyes were bright with delight.

Aidan steered them toward the changing room—thankfully on the opposite side of the studio from the women's.

"I don't have the slightest clue what you're talking about, Mack."

"You're joshing me, aren't you, Doc?" Mack punched him playfully in the arm with one of his meat-cleaver-sized fists. That would bruise. "As one of the Inseparables, you don't have a clue?"

"The Inseparables?" Now Aidan actually *didn't* know what Mack was talking about.

"You and Harty. Do you think the rest of us are blind?"

Mack waited for him to catch up but Aidan refused to play along, giving him a blank look in return as he pushed through the doors into the changing room.

"Always with each other? At training? Out of training? You don't get one without the other? C'mon, Doc. You and your last assistant never hung out that much. Just how many 'work dinners' does a guy need?"

"It's the lead-up to the finals." Aidan pressed his lips together. He wasn't so sure he liked where this was going.

"Ali and Aidan, sitting on a tree..." Mack was really getting into the swing of things now.

"All right! I get your point! Go take a shower, you rank beast."

"Hey, Aidan!" another player shouted from the doorway. "Harty wants to know if she should wait for you after to grab some dinner?"

Mack shot Aidan a knowing look, snapped him

with a towel and ran toward the showers, hooting with triumphant glee.

Cringeworthy didn't even *begin* to cover it. The half dozen or so players who'd joined them for the class all turned to him, waiting for his answer.

Of *course* he wanted to meet her for dinner. And pudding. And every single meal in between now and the end of her three-month contract. Not that he'd tell them—or her. But blowing her off in front of the guys...? That wasn't cool.

He scanned their expectant faces. This truly was a no-win situation. Blow her off and retain his 'The Monk' moniker, or accept the invitation and open himself up to some top-rate razzing.

He was man enough. He could do this.

"Tell her I'll meet her outside in fifteen. I need to talk over some of your body fat charts with her." *Good cover, Aidan.*

Whoops of delight mingled with some not so subtle catcalls as Aidan elbowed his way to his locker to grab a towel. Insufferable, these lads. Couldn't a fellow go out for an entirely innocent meal with a colleague?

As he tugged off his T-shirt he thought of Ali doing the same thing on that faraway night at the airport hotel, her eyes alive with desire. His body responding to her every move.

Maybe his thoughts weren't so innocent. He'd have to put a stop to their after-hours "mates" thing. And soon.

"You're acting weird tonight." Ali twisted her fork through her clam *spaghettini* and waggled the noodles at Aidan accusingly.

"*You're* acting weird," he retorted.

"Aidan." She put on her best schoolmarm voice. "I am not going to play *No, you are* with you all night. What's going on, weirdo?" She popped the forkful of food into her mouth with a smirk.

Aidan sighed and pushed back from the table. He wasn't hungry, and that meant only one thing. He was about to do something he didn't feel right about. The only way he could keep this relationship verging on anything close to professional was to put a halt to these out-of-work get-togethers. They could cloak them in any guise they wanted—exercise, going over notes, getting a bite to eat, watching replays of the game—but at the end of the day he and Ali were spending time together because they liked it. *He liked it.*

Even watching television seemed an empty experience if she wasn't there, wondering aloud why on earth he had to keep flicking the channels so much or have the volume on "so freakin' loud." How this had come to pass in a few short weeks was beyond him, but if the team was calling them The Inseparables they weren't far off base.

"Hey, what's wrong?" Ali's expression was genuinely concerned now, nothing remaining of her goofy grin.

"You want it straight up or watered down?"

A small crease formed between her eyes. He didn't blame her. He was being elusive, and the only person his behavior was protecting was himself.

Nipping this thing with Ali in the bud was the kindest way to go. She might as well go forward with her eyes wide open.

"It's nothing, really…" He dove in, avoiding eye contact by rearranging his ravioli into a poor recreation of a St. George's Cross. "The guys were just giving me some guff after our 'cross-training' and they seem to think we're a couple. I just don't want them to get the wrong idea—you know…with the final coming up and all. *Focus*.

They need to focus. *I* need to focus—make sure they don't get injured—and *you* need—"

*Quit talking.*

She put her fork down quietly. "I see."

"None of this hanging out together has been romantic, right?" He raised his eyes hopefully.

"Of course not!" She huffed away the very idea. "What on earth would make them think I fancy you?"

Ali regretted the words the moment they were out of her mouth. There were about five gabillion things that would make the team, let alone Aidan, think she fancied him—but she really didn't need to put them in outline form for him to analyze.

"That came out wrong."

"You think?" Aidan's voice was dryer than the Sauvignon Blanc he'd just taken a sip of.

"Soooo…" She folded her serviette and laid it on the table. Her appetite had been properly stemmed. No wine, and now no pudding. "What exactly do you propose we do to set them right?"

She glared at Aidan. This was completely his fault. If he hadn't sent her that Cosmopolitan all those weeks ago none of this would be happening. Right?

*Wrong.*

It most likely wouldn't have mattered *where* she'd met Aidan Tate. He knocked her for six on or off the field. They had chemistry, and trying to ignore it was going to be a Herculean task.

"Well, we can't exactly stop working together— Coach is insisting you stay." Aidan frowned.

"Wow. Thanks for the vote of confidence," Ali snapped back.

Unexpectedly, Aidan laughed. "I suppose this sort of thing isn't really a problem at your clinic, with all those girlies floating about in their tutus."

*"Nothing* at my clinic is like being here," Ali grumbled.

"Hey." Aidan reached across and gave her hand a squeeze. "It's not *all* bad up here, is it?"

"Better watch it. What if someone from the team sees you?"

Ali pulled her hand back, knowing she was milliseconds away from weaving her fingers through his, finding comfort in the warmth of his hand. But comfort was the last thing she could expect from Aidan. He was making sure she knew that—loud and clear.

"C'mon, Ali. Don't be like that."

"Like what? There's obviously nothing going on between us—so we're good." She gave him a cheery smile. "I'll get the bill. Or do you want to go Dutch so no one gets the wrong idea?"

"Now you're just being childish."

"Childish? Really? I'm trying to play this game by your ever-changing rulebook, Aidan. Apologies if I'm not managing to keep up."

"I'm just trying to make this easy."

Aidan gave her a pointed look with those dark brown eyes of his. Eyes that were just far too close to those deliciously strong cheekbones, so prominent you could trace them oh-so-easily straight down to his mouth. She felt her focus narrowing. He really had a lovely mouth...

An unwelcome warmth started to make itself known between her legs. She shifted in her seat. And all of a sudden it came to her—clear as day. She had the perfect solution. "I've got it."

"What?"

"How we fix this 'thing.'" Her fingers hung in the air in quotes as her heart began to race with excitement. This could *really* work! She looked him square in the eye. "The easiest thing to do would be to start having sex again, so we can quit pretending that being pals is what we both want. I like working with you—but this whole buddy thing is a farce. We should be... I don't know... booty call buddies instead."

Ali clapped her hand over her mouth, astonished she'd said the words out loud.

Aidan sat silently for a moment, just watching her. He looked down at his hands, then back up at her, his face a picture of sobriety.

"All right, then."

"What?" Ali's heart-rate took off. "What *exactly* are you saying all right to?"

She couldn't tear her eyes away from Aidan as she waited for him to answer. Had she—*they*—gone completely raving mad? Were they going to *do* this? Give being a couple a try? *No.* Booty call buddies. Having secret assignations in the night. This wasn't part of the plan. But feeling alive was, and if there was one thing she knew it was that being in Aidan's arms made her feel ridiculously alive. So...since that was the case... some regular sex might make it easier to ignore him at work. *Maybe.*

"Let's do it." He nodded his head decisively. "On one condition."

"Of course there's a condition." It was all Ali could do not to slap the table in frustration. "Jeez Louise, Aidan! Is *nothing* straightforward with you?"

He started laughing. *"Jeez Louise?"*

"Yeah—Jeez Louise." She started to giggle along with him. "Now, stop your laughing and tell me what your stupid condition is."

"How do you know it's stupid?"

"Because it's a condition on having yours truly as a friend with benefits—and with half the team proposing to me on a regular basis that's just stupid. Like you."

Maybe she should poke him in the arm for good measure. She was enjoying this now. *Friends with benefits.* She'd never done that before. Tick! An unexpected add-on to her list of new activities. Would she regret this later? Most likely. Then again—nothing ventured...

"We keep it like it was at the airport."

"What? No names? I think we're a bit late for that."

"I was thinking more along the lines of what goes on on the road stays..." He let her fill in the blanks.

*Hmm...* She could see where he was coming from. Getting non-stop shtick from the team could be tricky if they went public about things.

"Not even my gal pals Down South?" Not that she really had anyone to fit that role—but being a sort-of couple with the sexiest man alive...? She needed to tell *someone*!

"Not even them. Loose lips and all that..."

"Until when?"

"The end of your contract."

"Then this 'friendship' ends?" She indicated the two of them with a quick flick of her hand.

"Precisely."

Now Aidan was smiling, as well. One of those sultry come-hither numbers. Tingles of anticipation began to slow-dance across her nerve endings. She needed to get this show on the road, *stat*.

"Do you want it in writing?"

"I can think of quite a few other ways we can seal the deal." Aidan gave her a decidedly saucy look.

Ali tucked her lips in, then pushed them out decisively. If she'd thought she was numb to the world's delights before she'd come Up North, she was swinging giddily straight to the other side of the pendulum.

"Very well, then." She extended her hand across the table to shake on it. "I'm ready when you are, Suit."

"Miss Cosmopolitan."

He took her hand carefully, almost studiously in his, bent and pressed his lips upon it before looking up from her fingers with a naughty, naughty, grin.

"Waiter! Check, please."

To have said the walk back to Aidan's flat was fraught with sexual tension would have been putting it mildly. She'd never had such an openly agreed upon fling without strings. Then again, she had never physically ached to be with someone as much as she desired Aidan. *Never.*

After her mum had died she'd pretty much perfected being one of life's cooler customers. A few dates here. A few dates there. By choice she'd never had anything to really dig her teeth into. Not to say that she hadn't bitten Aidan's shoulder, trying to stop herself from unleashing a non-hotel-friendly howl of rapture. Or scratched his back with her nails. Maybe just a little. And he had groaned with pleasure.

Oh, she was in trouble. If her all-over body tingling was anything to go by, the veneer was threatening to crack.

*No.* No it wasn't. This was just overdue, right? A sexy encounter. It would make everything easier. More relaxed.

Aidan brushed his hand against the back of hers, then wove his fingers through hers as they virtually race-walked through the narrow brick passage leading to their riverside complex. A whoosh of electricity shot through her.

*Long, long overdue.*

She snuck a peek at him. Blimey, he was good-looking. Would it be acceptable to just jump on him right now? There weren't that many people walking along the river on this cold March night. Maybe here, in the dark of the passageway? A perfect place for secret lovers to share a kiss. Or a thousand. Not that they *were* lovers. They were— Well... She didn't know what they were. She couldn't remember ever wanting someone as much as she had ached for Aidan's touch. And then to have to put it on hold for the past few weeks... She'd needed every single one of those kickboxing classes. Aidan had been right. She had energy to burn.

"Everything all right?" He gave her hand a quick squeeze before letting go of it to dig a key out of his pocket.

Ali felt her entire body tingling with desire. She watched as he put the key in the door and licked her lips in anticipation of what was to come.

They were here. Outside the door of his flat. In a manner of microseconds she could start ripping off his clothes and sating the hunger she hadn't appreciated just how much she'd been stemming. Everything was more than all right. Everything was set to just get better and better. As long as she could keep her heart in check everything would be perfect.

"Wow." Ali wasn't sure if she'd whispered the word or just mouthed it.

"You can say that again." Aidan nuzzled into her neck and threw in some kisses along her shoulder for good measure. *Yum.*

*"Wooooooowwwwwuhhh!"* She whooshed the sound into his ear, gave him a few kiss-nibbles

along his jawline, then turned her head toward the starlit view. "Do you think people can see in?"

Aidan was still holding her up against his floor-to-ceiling windows, her legs wrapped around his waist, her body as bare as the day she'd come into the world. Just like his. She felt as if they'd just had naughty hotel sex, minus the hotel.

"Not at three in the morning."

Ali unfolded her legs and started gathering up her erratically scattered clothes.

"Is that what time it is? I had no idea. What time do we have to be at the stadium?"

"Cool your jets. Coach Stone called me yesterday, and as it's Saturday they're doing some sort of cross-country run in the morning, then meeting with their nutritionist and calling it a day at lunchtime. We're just on call tomorrow. Today." He corrected.

"Thanks for telling me, boss." She glared at him, did a quick calculation and dropped her clothes back on the floor. "Sooooo..." She sauntered back over to him with a sexual confidence she'd never known she possessed. "We've got time for a snooze."

"We've got time for a lot of things."

Aidan grabbed her by the hand and pulled her over to his big ol' Man Bed, complete with dark navy duvet and sheets in that weird Merlot color men always seemed to like. His interior décor skills, however, were the least of her concerns. Everyone had to have a flaw. Let that be his.

She snuggled into his arms as if she'd been doing it every day for the past five years. What a sea change! She would never have dreamed it was possible to have such open and trusting sex with someone—let alone hanging around for a snuggle…

Ali tugged Aidan's top arm more snugly round her waist and wove her fingers through his. Safe and secure. That was how she felt. Which was hilarious, considering it was the last thing she should be feeling with this obvious commitment-phobe. The hours they'd just shared had definitely topped their time at the airport. Aidan seemed to know her body better than she did. Intimacy with him was— *Rewind!* This wasn't intimacy. It was what they'd agreed on: a couple of months of blissful commitment-free sex. And then—and then what?

*Then you move on to something else, like you always do.*

Besides, who knew what the world would be waiting to throw on her plate next week, let alone in a few months' time?

Aidan's breath slowed and with it the cadence of her own breathing steadied. *Right now*, she thought as she felt herself slipping off to sleep... *Right now is good.*

"It's a gorgeous day out there." Aidan took a slurp of Ali's thick-as-tar version of coffee and winced. Blimey. If he judged her coffee in the same vein as her lovemaking there didn't seem to be a single thing this woman didn't do by halves. "What do you say I take you on a tour of the River Teal?"

"Are there footpaths?" Ali raised an interested eyebrow and took a deep drink from her coffee mug without a trace of a flinch. She was clearly made of tougher stuff than he was.

"Miles of them. So I thought it would be more fun if we went by bike. There's a rental shop just round the corner—or, if you like, you could go wild and buy one."

"Ah..." Ali's enthusiastic expression cooled.

"There's a really nice gastropub about ten or fifteen miles down from here—straight along the river. We could earn ourselves a really nice lunch."

"Anything we could *walk* to? I'm game for a hike!"

"It's flat, if that's what's got you all frowny."

"I'm not worried about not being able to make it, Aidan. I just wondered if there were any good walks instead."

Aidan hesitated. There was something going on here that wasn't about foot or cycle paths.

"There are loads of walks, but the White Hart is a really special place—I'd love to take you there. It's great to approach it from the riverside."

"Maybe another time." Ali peered out the window and pointed out some nonexistent clouds. "Looks like the weather could turn at any time. We wouldn't want to be stuck out in bad weather in March."

"Dr. Ali Lockhart—if I didn't know better I would think you didn't know how to ride a bike."

From the wounded expression that immediately appeared on her face Aidan guessed he'd hit the nail on the head. He reached across and gave her arm a reassuring rub.

"Not to worry. I can teach you how to ride. With all of your yoga panache you should pick it up easily."

"No." Her voice was brittle and she gave him a look laced with nothing less than gritty ire. "I know how to ride a bike, thanks. I just don't *want* to ride a bike."

"Hey, you." Aidan came out from behind the kitchen island and gave her arm a gentle squeeze. "We don't have to do anything you don't want to, but from what I've seen you're game for just about anything. What's so off-putting about jumping on a bicycle?"

Ali fought the urge to turn away from him and pressed her lips tightly shut. It was her go-to reaction whenever anyone tried to get closer—to "talk things out." She didn't do close. How could Aidan come anywhere near understanding how utterly hollowed out she'd felt when her mum had been taken from her? She trusted Aidan implicitly on an intimate sexual level. Could she trust him to understand the workings of her heart?

She pressed her eyes shut for a count of three,

then opened them up. Yup. He was still there, a gentle smile of encouragement playing on his lips. Maybe it would be good for her. Part of the go-on-the-road psychological reboot she was trying to give herself. If she told Aidan, perhaps she could leave all of the grief she felt behind when she went back home. Not to mention the fact she felt a really overwhelming urge to tell him.

"My mum and I..." She paused and took a deep, steadying breath.

She shouldn't have gulped her coffee down so quickly. Then again, maybe the caffeine would help get everything out. Quickly.

She stared into her mug and began again. "I was raised by my mum. My dad turned out not to be 'The One' she thought he was, but she didn't let it get her down. She was a champion. An amazing woman who worked her socks off to make sure my dreams of becoming a dancer could be fulfilled."

She looked up at Aidan, who nodded at her to continue. He pulled over a chair and plonked himself in it. The gesture said: *I'm not going anywhere. I'm here for you.*

Ali fought the tingling prick of tears and continued. In for a penny… "Anyway, my mum died of cancer when I was sixteen and—" She stopped, desperate to stem the sob that came with the memory. She swigged back a couple gulps of coffee and went on. "A few days after she died… As you can imagine, I wasn't really operating in the real world, but she'd made me promise that no matter what I would continue with my dancing. She believed in me and was convinced I'd be a prima ballerina one day. So, a few days after she died I was riding my bike to rehearsal—I was attending the British Ballet School on scholarship—and—"

"What happened?" Aidan nodded for her to continue, giving her elbow a quick squeeze. He was there for her. He would help her carry the load.

"A couple of streets—" Ali grabbed the counter edge and dug her nails in until they went white from the pressure. "A couple of streets away from the school I was sideswiped by a lorry."

Aidan clapped a hand over his mouth. She could see he knew what was next, but she pointed to the scars on her knee anyhow.

"No more ballet for Ali." Her eyes met his.

"Oh, Ali. I am *so* sorry for your loss." And he looked as though he truly meant it."

"I just wish for my mum's sake I had become a dancer. Made her dream come true!"

"Wasn't it your dream, as well?"

"Yes, but—" She stopped, realizing she'd never really bothered to look at from that angle before. "I suppose once I found medicine I found something else I loved."

"Isn't that enough? Don't you think your mother would be bursting with pride to know her daughter not only overcame her accident but had the strength to be a—no, *the* leading specialist in dance injuries?"

"I hadn't really thought of it like that." Despite her best efforts, she felt tears fill her eyes. "I just miss her so much."

She abruptly cleared her throat and swiped at her eyes. This was all too close to the bone. Too much like opening up your heart to someone who was going to stick around. Neither she nor Aidan were going down that road, so she'd be best to cut this conversation off now.

"So. In answer to the question, Do I think a

bike ride would be a fun thing to do? No, I really, *really* don't."

He gave her a sad smile and nodded his understanding, before putting a hand on her knee and rubbing his thumb along one of her scars.

Her gut instinct was to bridle. And then something inside her shifted. In a good way. For the first time it felt as though she was just *saying* the words she'd repeated again and again after losing so much. *I don't want to ride a bicycle.* Had she really meant them this time? Was she ready to tackle this demon?

Aidan leaned back against the counter with a studied look. "I can't even imagine how horrible that must've been, but I've got to ask—are you not bike-riding because you blame yourself for having the accident in the first place, or because you're scared?"

"How do you *do* that?" Ali couldn't believe her ears.

"What?"

"Take something that's been gnawing me up from the inside out for a long time and boil it down to two simple questions?"

It was difficult to tell if she felt angry or relieved. As she sought answers in his eyes Ali felt her chest release its tight grip on her lungs and her shoulders dropped a little. Relaxed back into place.

"Probably because I'm not living it," Aidan replied. "Perspective is a whole lot easier if you're not the one busy slaying dragons."

*Good point.*

"Is that the voice of experience talking?"

"Perhaps." He shrugged. "We've all got demons stuffed in our closets, don't we?" He looked away for a moment, his eyes fixed on an invisible horizon, then turned back to her with a bright smile. "But I bet you'd look damn hot in dragon-slaying getup." He gave her a wink, grabbed her empty mug and moved to the sink to wash up.

Ali couldn't help herself. She smiled. A picture of herself in a warrior-princess outfit—or maybe a slinky chainmail number—flashed across her mind's eye. Sword in hand, fire-breathing dragon backing down as she fearlessly approached.

Her eyebrows moved closer together as she concentrated on Aidan's questions. *Yes.* Yes, she supposed she *did* blame herself, to an extent. Her mentor at the dance academy had spent countless hours assuring her that her mother would never have minded a jot. Her only goal had been to make sure Ali was happy. And yet here she was, still slaying dragons all by herself. No mum. No one she felt brave enough to open up her heart to.

She looked over at Aidan, giving the mugs a good scrub. Maybe she had a little help now. Could she go forward and let go of her unful-filled dreams? Perhaps create some new ones?

Maybe.

Would never riding a bike again change the fact that the plan they had spoken about again and again as her mother's health had failed would never be a reality?

Ali traced a figure-eight pattern along the ta-bletop. "Are these paths completely closed to traf-fic?"

"Completely," Aidan replied solidly, popping the clean mugs one by one onto the draining board. "And I've got two very large, deeply un-attractive helmets and reflective vests we will *both* wear. At all times. Even at lunch."

"And does this gastropub you're talking about have sticky toffee pudding?" She had to hold out just a little bit. Didn't she?

"With honeycomb ice cream on the side."

"Now you're talking!"

Ali slid off of her stool and walked over to Aidan. She couldn't help it. She needed a hug. As if reading her mind, he turned away from the sink, slipped his arms around her waist and popped a little kiss on her forehead. She nestled up against his chest and let herself breathe him in. Friends gave each other a cuddle every now and again, right? Even friends who had spent the bulk of the night exploring one another's bodies in just about the most erotic way possible?

She stilled her own breathing. If you took away the physical attraction she had for him, she was still left with a huge mountain of respect. Professionally and—the more she was getting to know him—personally. Aidan's chin rested lightly on the top of her head and in the quiet of the morning she could hear his heartbeat.

Even though she knew this whole thing—whatever it was—was temporary, was just "matey," she felt safe, cared for. Protected. Was this what it felt like to let someone in? Of course, there was a time limit with Aidan. They'd shaken hands on it. That kind of deal was binding. Just a couple of months. Just enough time to get ready to move on.

"Want to run over to yours and change?" Aidan moved his chin off of her head and took a glance at his watch. "I'll meet you by the river in ten minutes."

"And if after two minutes I decide I want to back out and come home...?"

"I've got a few unopened box sets waiting to be watched." He rubbed his palms together gleefully.

"What kind?"

"Zombies, intergalactic warzones and old Westerns."

Ali couldn't help the crinkle of dismay from appearing on her face. *Yuck!* Not her genres in any way. Okay. Deep breath. She could do this. Bike-riding it was.

"See you in ten."

# CHAPTER SIX

"Do you see those swans up ahead? Lovely, aren't they?"

"Sure are!" Ali was laughing now.

Aidan had been playing the distraction game non-stop since they'd hit the bicycle path, and by this point he knew his psychological tactics were well and truly transparent.

He was proud of her. Seriously, right into the marrow of his bones proud. When they'd started out, just wheeling the bikes across the street at a traffic crossing, she had looked whiter than a ghost. Rosy cheeks and glittering blue eyes wouldn't even begin to describe the energy pouring from her now. He would like to think he'd had a small part in helping her, but she was a strong woman. She would've reached this place on her own eventually.

Sometimes getting a small push in the right direction was all you needed. Too bad *he* couldn't take a dose of the same medicine. Maybe then he'd be open to the possibility of love again. Too bad life just hadn't handed him the right cards.

He glanced across at Ali. She was grinning away at the swans circling at the river's edge. It was going to be hard to say goodbye when the time came.

"Pub's not too far beyond them."

"Aidan Tate! That's exactly what you said after the locks, after the chestnut trees, and after the ducks! I'm beginning to think this pub is a bit of fiction on your part."

Aidan looked at her as if he were aghast she could suggest such a thing. "I have done no such thing! Look." He pointed ahead as a gabled roof just started to become visible in the distance. "I can smell the sticky toffee from here. Race you?"

"You're on."

Ali would know if he let her win, so the only fair thing to do would be to give her a run for her money. Head bent, stomach muscles tightened, he began to press the pedals of his bike with all the welly he could muster.

"This has to be the gooiest pudding I've ever had." Ali put the spoon back in her mouth, knowing that until she had devoured every last drop of toffee she just wouldn't, in good conscience, be able to leave the table. It would be rude to the chef not to lick the plate absolutely clean. Fifteen miles on a bike—not ten!—was worth every calorie-loaded morsel.

"You could always eat the plate." Aidan's voice was ripe with sarcasm.

"Hey, mister!" Ali waggled the shiny clean spoon at him. "This whole thing was your idea. You should feel proud all of your brainwashing worked. The dragon has been slayed."

As she spoke the words she realized there just might be some truth in them. She would always miss her mother. Deeply so. But burying herself in her work would never bring her back, no matter how hard she tried. Nor would moving on every time she felt as if she just might be getting a friend—or in this case a lover. But she wasn't quite ready to go there yet. This "friends with benefits" thing would do for now. Even so, today felt like a bit of a breakthrough—almost as if she was looking at the world through a fresh lens.

"I'm delighted to hear it, O Warrior Princess." Aidan gave her a wink before trying to steal a bit more pudding. Unsuccessfully.

"Thank you." Ali locked eyes with him.

"For what? Letting you eat all of my pudding as well as your own?"

"Don't be coy. You know as well as I do I might never have ridden a bike again if it weren't for you."

Aidan leaned his elbows on the table, resting his chin on the weave of his fingers. "As much as I would love to bask in the glory of your leap forward in the cycling world, I am quite convinced the bulk of the credit lies on your side of the table."

"How do you work that out? You're the one who suggested the bike ride."

"You're the one who got on the bike."

Ali felt her lips stretch into a huge grin. "I did, didn't I?" She swiped the spoon in a Zorro-esque X gesture, scooped up the last bite of pudding and then airplaned it over to Aidan. "I suppose it'll still be a wait-and-see-what-happens when I get back to London...not so sure about the busy streets there. But I still think I owe you a thank-you."

"Well, this will do nicely." Aidan took the spoon from her hand and consumed the enormous mouthful in one fell swoop, eyes staying with hers as he finished it with a satisfied cartoon gulp. "Are you looking forward to going back?"

*Not really. Best dodge that one.*

"It'll be interesting to see what my colleague has done to my practice."

"That's a lot of trust to put into someone."

"Cole Manning is my Old Reliable in the friend department. We went to med school together."

"Surely you've got a stack of those?"

"No."

Aidan leaned back in his chair. "You sound pretty certain about that."

Ali sighed and tipped her head into her hands, taking her time to run her thumbs along her temples before looking back up. This man was intent on digging up all her old baggage today, wasn't he? She was in a great mood, feeling proud, and churning up those dark days, when she'd shut just about everyone who cared for her out of her life… *Ugh.* She'd done enough dragon-slaying for the day.

"I think I've done more than enough baring of my soul today. Maybe it's time I turned the tables?" She shot him an impish grin.

"Fancy some banoffee pie before we hit the road? Potassium is good fuel!"

Ali laughed. "Nice conversation-changer, Tate!"

Fair enough. Maybe he didn't have any old baggage. Then again...that was unlikely. Everyone had baggage—it just came in different shapes and sizes. She'd play along and give Aidan a break. She owed him one for today. Big-time.

"I think I've probably eaten more than the entire ballet company at this one sitting! Ballerinas don't really do puddings. Nor do gymnasts. It's been great being around people who eat!"

"What made you pick dance injuries as your specialty?"

"It sort of evolved, I guess. No. That's not right. I'd made my mum a promise. She dedicated her life to helping me reach *my* dream, so I thought it was only right that I help other dancers reach theirs. A karma balancer, I guess."

He nodded, eyebrows lifted with approval.

"So, you're totally on your own now?"

"Yup. That about sums it up! What about you?"

Now she really *did* need to switch the tables. Ali felt a fresh sting of tears tickling at the back of her throat. Their day together had been so great—it'd be a shame to mess it up now.

"Oh, you know…" Aidan looked off toward the fire burning in the far corner of the pub.

"No, I don't. That's why I asked you." Ali tried to be playful with her taunt but could see there was a lot of hidden history in those eyes of his. Not from anything she'd caused, but there was hurt lurking in there somewhere.

There was definitely more to this man than being an über-confident charm machine who picked up girls at airports. She'd learned that over and over again from the team. They respected him. Why on earth someone so talented, not to mention big and bouncy-balloon-gorgeous was single was beyond her.

"What do you say we race home, get back into bed and watch one of those box sets?" Aidan crumpled up his paper serviette and popped it on to the table.

*And the crowd goes wild at yet another artful dodge by Dr. Aidan Tate!*

"I think I'll leave the zombies to you. I've got a couple of exciting loads of laundry to catch up on." She reached across the table and gave his hand a squeeze. If she was going to keep her heart sewed up tight, twenty-four-seven with Aidan Tate was simply not an option. "But, Aidan, seriously, I want to thank you for today. I didn't think I'd ever be on a bike saddle again, and you've just helped me tick off one of my New Year's resolutions!"

"Which one was that?"

"'Poke Your Demons in the Eye'—number seventeen," she answered without a moment's hesitation.

Aidan laughed heartily. It was nice to see the smile back on his face. Maybe one day he'd rate her as someone he could confide in in the same way he'd been there for her.

He pushed his chair back and grabbed his bicycle helmet off of the adjacent chair. Today obviously wasn't going to be "one day."

"Just how many of these resolutions do you have to get through?"

Ali felt a light flush color her cheeks. She might just possibly have gone a bit overboard in the resolutions department.

"Seventy-three."

*"Ha!"* Aidan hooted to the ceiling. "And you've done *one*? Harty—you've got a lot of work to do."

"Oh, I've done at least two!" she shot back, before she thought better of it.

"Oh, *reeeeally*?"

He drew out the second word, making it all smoky...sexy. *Sheeesh.* Did the man do *anything* that didn't make her want to rip his clothes off?

"Yes," she responded primly.

"And what exactly was this other resolution?"

"Well, it wasn't 'Have a One-Night Stand at the Airport With the Man Who is Your New Boss.'" She popped on her helmet and snapped the straps together with a flourish. "It was 'Try New Things.'"

Aidan put his hand in the small of her back as they headed toward the riverside exit to the pub. "I see. So, what new things did you try?"

"I had a one-night stand at the airport with the man who it turned out was my new boss."

Would he take that hand off the small of her back? She was feeling sassy. *Super*-sassy. She made a beeline for her bicycle, which was chained to a railing at the river's edge.

"Sounds exciting." Aidan was right behind her, his breath teasing along the length of her neck.

"It was."

He turned her around to face him. *Heavenly bodies*, he knew how to unleash the butterflies. His fingers brushed her cheek as he unclipped her helmet, removed it and pulled her close to him in one incredibly fluid move. Didn't this kind of thing only happen in movies?

"The guy must've been something special. To catch the eye of a girl like you."

He tipped her chin up with a finger and her eyes caught the hungry look in his.

"Oh, he was all right..." she managed to whisper. Whimper was more like it.

"Sounds like he had room for improvement." Aidan's mouth began a torturously slow descent toward her own.

"Like I said, he's all right..." Her voice faded away.

When their lips finally met Ali felt a rush of desire surge through her so powerfully she could hardly believe it was real. The kiss was soft, tender, and then passionately loaded with all the triumph and depth of feeling she'd experienced that day. And yet—it was just a kiss.

Just a kiss? That'd be like calling Rudolph Nureyev *just* a chap who wore tights. If they hadn't been in public she probably would've torn Aidan's fleece and everything else off him right then and there. Not that he brought out the wild animal in her or anything. Or that it was part of their "deal."

"Well, then!" Ali pulled back from Aidan, using the railing as ballast. "Guess we better get you back to your box sets!"

Aidan dropped another one of those flirty winks in her direction. "I'd hate to keep you from your laundry."

*Oh, we're getting to the laundry, all right! Just the emotional kind. And it feels an awful lot like the spin cycle!*

# CHAPTER SEVEN

"So, HAVE THINGS improved with Tate?"

*In a manner of speaking...*

"They're going all right." Ali crossed her fingers, relieved that her friend and new head of En Pointe couldn't see her face. She was a terrible liar. They were having their weekly "clinic catchup" chat, and keeping Aidan off of the topic list was getting harder.

"When I worked with him he was definitely a hard nut to crack—definitely keeps himself to himself—but I thought you two would hit it off."

*That's one way to put it.*

Better stay on safer territory. "So, what have you done to my practice? How has the team taken to your new-fangled American ways?"

"Oh, I'd say I've been dragging this little house that Ali built into the twenty-first century!"

"What?" Ali sat bolt-upright. She had a Class A clinic and knew as well as her former classmate did that it was miles ahead of other clinics in the city, let alone the country. He was lucky she trusted him so much.

"Chillax, Lockhart. Don't worry. I've actually dragged it back a few centuries. One of the girls—the Russian one—"

"Which Russian one? There are heaps of them!" Ali couldn't help but laugh.

"I don't know—Katarina, Alexandra, Olga—*anyhooooow...*" Cole Manning drew out the word in his usual leisurely Southern drawl. The man sure could drag out a story. "I got an acupuncturist in to help her with some of the tendonitis. Seems to have made a difference."

"That's great! It's probably Alexandra—the ballet doesn't have many Olgas. At least not the way you say it."

"How *do* I say it?" Cole was laughing now, too.

"Like anyone called Olga is a troll. Does she have long blond hair?"

"What do you want from me, Ali? They've all either got long blond or long black hair. The least you could've done was color-code them a bit more for me!"

"Listen, mister!" Ali cried, despite the laughter

burbling away in her throat. "If you mess with my clinic—"

"Hold on, girl. Don't you mean *my* clinic? That was the deal, wasn't it? I get you a top locum position Up North and you keep your mitts off while I have my wicked way with En Pointe— Britain's number one destination for ballerinas and gymnasts on the mend."

"Cole Manning—you just remember I have put my life's work into that place. If you—"

"Easy, there, tiger. I'm only messing with you. Everything's fine. The clients are fine—the list is growing, in fact."

"What? Who?" Ali sat up straight. She loved a new challenge as much as the next doctor, but equally she knew all of the local prima ballerinas personally—and a new client meant a new injury. An injury that could spell the end of a career.

"Erm—let me have a look."

She could hear papers being shuffled across a desk. "You haven't made my—*your*—desk a complete pigsty, have you, Cole?"

Ali grinned at the phone as she spoke the words. Of course he had. The man was a certified genius—but he scored in the negatives when it came to tidiness. So much for the "tidy desk, tidy mind" adage.

"Look, Little Miss Everything Has Its Correct Time and Place, I thought this whole switcheroo was to shake things up a bit?"

"Yeah, but—"

"Yeah, but nothin'." Now Cole was serious. "You did *not* trek up to the far North of England and surround yourself with a bunch of testosterone-laden menfolk just to keep everything clinical and perfect like you always do."

"I hardly think—"

"That's precisely your problem, Ali. You think too much. Stop it. Live a little, why don'tcha?"

*If only he knew.*

"You're lucky you said all that with your cute Southern accent, Cole. Otherwise, I might have half a mind to come down and clean up my— *your*—desk right now," she playfully sniped back.

But his words had the sting of truth about them. Then again, one-night stands, kickboxing and having a time and date-stamped affair were all pretty big steps in the Leaping Emotional Hurdles department, right?

\* \* \*

Aidan couldn't resist. He lightly traced his finger along the lock of hair shading Ali's sleeping face and tucked it back behind her ear. Fourteen. That was the number of light freckles that made up a tiny constellation across her nose. Two. The number of nibbly, kissable, lush lips he was currently trying to resist. Two. The number felt leaden now. The number of weeks left in Ali's contract.

He gave her cheek a stroke with the back of his hand and rolled onto his back, his arm still trapped by her head.

She was a snuggler. And he had to admit he was loving every wiggly, cuddly, close-as-you-can-get moment of being with her. And it wasn't just the sex. Make no mistake—the sex was good. Ridiculously good. But Ali was the whole package, and as the days wore on—or ran out—he was feeling less and less like this whole "what goes on the road, stays on the road" affair was fair.

Ali deserved more. Someone who would— *could*—open up his heart and giftwrap her in lashings of love. Deep, full-bodied love.

Two weeks. That was all they had left. Two

weeks until the big North-South match. It was something he had never thought he'd dread.

If what he'd had with Ali had only been that one extraordinary night at the hotel, then saying goodbye would have been much easier. She would definitely have been etched on his mind forever, and heaven knew going to the airport would never be a straightforward business again, but one night with this amazing woman would have been survivable.

Now, with the few dozen nights they'd already notched up… Total annihilation. She'd nabbed him—hook, line and sinker. Getting over Ali at this juncture was going to be near on impossible. Which was why he had to start closing the doors.

"Are you watching me sleep?" Ali cracked a single eye open, her fingers taking a lazy journey across his chest.

"Hardly!" He protested with a grin. "That would be creepy."

"Yes." She nodded in sleepy agreement. "That would. It's not like you'd be falling for me, or anything daft like that."

*Okay, mind reader. Enough of that.*

"Got it in one," he replied lightly, as if feigning falling in love would hide the reality.

"Yeah, right." She replied with a cheeky grin. "As if The Monk would fall for his fluffy ballerina locum."

"Stranger things have happened." He was straining to keep his voice bright. "What are you up to today?"

"I was thinking of going into town to buy a lamp." She pushed herself up on an elbow and began to thoughtfully trace a finger along his shoulder. "I only have the one, and I have to keep dragging it from the lounge into the bedroom when I want to read in bed."

Aidan laughed. "It's a bit late in the game to be making yourself at home, isn't it?"

"That's rich, coming from you." She gave him a poke in the chest.

"What's *that* supposed to mean?" He knew what it meant, but it'd be interesting to have Ali's take on his rather sparse décor.

"You had the gall to come to my place when I'd been there all of two weeks and mock my one-sofa, two-chair existence, only for me to discover you lived virtually the same way after—how many years has it been, Dr. Tate?"

"Five terribly busy years."

"Five years. And you have…let's see…two more lamps than I do and a better-stocked larder. Oh, and more throw pillows than you can shake a stick at," Ali teased, then fell back onto her pile of pillows. "If you like, I'll give you my new lamp when I go."

Aidan rolled over onto his back. He didn't want to think about that. Or discuss his own "bare bones" decorating style. Staring at the ceiling suddenly seemed less like being under the microscope.

"It's easier to clean. Easier to not get attached."

"And what are you not getting attached to? Bookshelves? Sets of drawers?" Ali's voice was still warm with humor, but he definitely felt the conversation train taking a different route.

"Things I can't have."

"Like what?"

"Oh, I don't know."

*You, for one.*

He bought himself some more time. "Settling in just always seemed too much hassle. My life is out there—" he pointed out the window in the direction of the stadium "—not in here. Why waste time on home furnishings when my real investment is with the team? When I initially signed on this job was the promise of something more permanent than anything I'd have with a patient in hospital. I'd really get to know the team. Learn and grow with them. Help them."

"It's a bit like that at my clinic."

"Yes, I suppose it would be. But with the team—I don't know. I guess I felt I was signing on for something bigger. Something lasting. And then one player gets transferred, another signs off with injuries, coaches switch teams..." He trailed off. This was all getting a bit heavy for a Sunday morning. "And before you know it, your second-in-command leaves and is replaced by a nymphomaniac from the South."

"Hey! I don't ever hear you saying no!" A full smile lit up Ali's eyes before she pulled Aidan's arm around her shoulder and plopped back down on to the pillow.

"Very true. Then again—you'll just be another thing to replace when you swan off back to the magical land of London." Aidan traced his fingers along Ali's arm.

"You'd better not replace me!"

"You're the one with the contract."

"You know what I mean. It will be strange—going back..."

Aidan bit back the urge to ask her to stay. To say she was welcome to extend their "deal" as long as she wanted.

"Don't be crazy—you can have anything you want back there."

"Not anything." All the playfulness had drained from Ali's voice.

"Of course." Aidan slapped his forehead. *What an idiot.* "Your mum."

"My mum..." Ali repeated softly. "I miss her more than anything in the world."

"I can imagine."

"Poor little me!" Ali's voice came out louder than she'd intended. This conversation had definitely veered toward Gloomsville. "All alone in the world!"

"You've got friends down South, right?"

Ali barked out a quick laugh, then put on a singsong voice. "The valuable resource of hindsight has allowed me to see that I have been a great boss—but not necessarily so good in the social skills department."

"And why is that, then?" Aidan kept his eyes

trained on the ceiling. Having this conversation with Ali's naked body semi-nestled into his was not familiar territory for him. Actually, having any sort of conversation with a naked woman beside him was relatively new. *Ali* new.

"Oh... I just couldn't count on..."

"Couldn't count on what?" Aidan pressed gently.

It was like a light bulb being pinged on. Ali suddenly saw the situation as clear as a bell. "I had friends, and a teacher-cum-mentor who took care of me after my mum died. Then he died when I was in uni, and I guess I just short-circuited. I didn't want friends anymore. I just wanted a family."

As the words came out of her mouth she wished she could reel them back in. What a thing to say in front of Mr. Can't-and-Won't-Commit!

"Which is why I've come Up North to work with a bunch of testosterone-laden athletes."

Aidan threw her a bemused look. "Does working with rugby players put you off having a family?"

"No!" She waved away his theory. "It pushes me out of my comfort zone. Reminds me there's no one to depend upon but myself."

"You've got me!" Aidan remonstrated.

"Ha!" Ali snorted. "For about two more weeks!" Had he not remembered the conditions surrounding their "friendship?" Work and play—two very separate things, with one very solid deadline.

"And then what? London?"

"Hmm. I'm not so sure about London. I guess I pack up my new lamp—if I ever get to the shops and buy one—or give it to you and see what's next."

"You wouldn't stick around? Stay Up North?" He made a stab at lifting his eyebrows with black-and-white movie star panache. "It'd be satisfying to know someone finally figured out things up here are better than in the big smoke."

"Who knows? What is this, anyway? The Northern Inquisition?" Ali filled the quiet space after her question with a laugh, wanting to escape the taut atmosphere their conversation had enshrouded them in.

She didn't want to leave. Not one bit. She was genuinely enjoying her work with the team and could easily see herself staying. But in two weeks the clock would run out and her days as medical practitioner to the North Stars would be over.

More to the point, her days with Aidan would be over. She was dreading saying goodbye, so ignoring it seemed the easiest way to go. Why play twenty questions?

"No, it's not an inquisition," Aidan drawled. "But I was wondering…"

"Wondering what?" Ali couldn't stop her heart from skipping a beat. Would he ask her to stay?

"I was actually wondering how I could pull my arm out from underneath your dead weight of a head so I could go meet my girls."

Ali's eyes popped wide open, and quickly she pushed herself upright and away from him. "*Excuse* me?"

"My girls. Didn't I tell you about them?"

Ali grabbed an armful of duvet and covered herself up, an expression of shock playing across her face. "I'm pretty sure I would've remembered if you'd told me about your *children*."

It was Aidan's turn to pop his eyes wide open. And then he started laughing. Hard.

"Not my children, silly! Well, I mean—yes—in a way…"

He didn't stop laughing and it was now officially irritating.

"This hasn't really come out the way I meant it to."

"*What* hasn't come out the way you meant it to, Aidan?"

Ali's steely-eyed gaze was hilarious. Aidan knew he could fix it right now if he wanted to—help her grimace relax into a smile. *So why wasn't he fixing it?* The silence between them was humming with emotion and with a blast of clarity he realized how easy it was to imagine having children...having a family with Ali. The two of them and one, two, three—however many didn't matter. But that sort of idyllic future wasn't meant for him. History had been all too clear about that one. Best put on the brakes. All this talk of family, putting down roots, had clearly unbalanced him. Best return to firmer ground. Get real.

"I coach a girls' rugby team. Twelve and under."

Ali's shoulders dropped back into place and—as he'd hoped—there was that smile of hers. The one that worked its way straight into his heart.

"But it's probably best you go on ahead with your lamp-shopping. You can't come along to practice as my g—" He stopped himself before he finished the sentence, knowing it was already too late.

"Come as your what?"

Ali's voice had turned investigative. He was making one hell of a hash of this.

"Nothing—don't worry. I don't really know what I was saying."

"Were you going to say *girlfriend*?"

She said the word as if it tasted of moldy cheese. Or, more accurately, as if the idea of her being his girlfriend was about as preposterous as things could get.

"No." *Uh, yes*—he had been going to say that.

"Aidan Tate! You were going to say *girlfriend*!"

"I was not!"

"What?" Ali changed tack and stuck out her lower lip, trying her best to make a monster face. "Is the idea so unappealing?"

He laughed, but couldn't stop the curl of uneasiness shifting around his gut. Of course it would be great—better than great—to have Ali as his girlfriend, but that wasn't how things worked. How *this* worked. They'd agreed. They'd shaken hands on it!

Ali's laughter broke through the silence. "I'm

just messing with you, Tate. I know you didn't mean that."

*I did. I do. I can't.*

"'Course not—I just meant I'm their coach, so you can't take the mick out of me in front of the girls. You're more than welcome to come, or you can wander off into town and lamp-shop to your heart's content. Your choice."

"Sure thing, ding-a-ling."

Ali pushed herself out of the bed and pulled on a T-shirt and some tracksuit bottoms. Aidan let himself get lost in the graceful flow of her movements. He started when she spoke again.

"I think I'll take a raincheck on judging your coaching skills."

"You know—I'd love for you to meet the girls. It's just…well… They're used to it just being me and them."

"Right. Fine."

Aidan was smart enough to know that when a woman said "fine" the situation was anything but. He was pretty sure he'd just stuck his foot in it. Big-time.

"I'll see you tomorrow at work." She gave him a wave and turned to go.

"Great. Or see you later?" Aidan gave a wave to her disappearing figure, before deflating against the bed's headboard and smacking himself on the head.

*Girlfriend.*

He hadn't let himself call any of the women he'd seen over the years a girlfriend. In truth, none of his "relationships" had warranted it. He'd made it clear as day that he wasn't one for long-term. And now here he was, tables turned, trying to convince himself—no, to convince Ali—that he didn't want her to be his girlfriend, when he knew deep in his heart that was all he wanted. All he wanted and more.

Ali stared at the recipe she'd ripped out of the Sunday paper. What was *braising* steak anyway? Could you get that at a butchers? Were butchers even open on a Sunday? How long did one "reduce" stock? Why weren't there more *details*? *Disasterville.* This was never going to happen.

She flicked the paper over to see what another option might be.

*Super Simple Pizza.*

Pizza! Perfect. She could do that. Easy-peasy.

She'd already cleaned her flat, done all the laundry and folded her clothes. Three times. Then she'd gone out shopping, totally forgetting what it was she'd left home for in the first place, and returned home empty-handed. To the darkness. When she'd remembered she had gone out for a lamp. Oh, and then she'd gone for a run by the river. A long one.

She was still buzzing with excess energy and needed to take things down a notch. Aidan always looked so relaxed when he cooked, so she thought she'd give it a whirl. Not that he was her go-to resource for how to fix a problem.

*Urrrrrrgh!*

She was tense. Shoulders-up-in-her-ears tense. The whole debacle that morning with Aidan over the word *girlfriend* just made her cringe.

She didn't know why she'd said it. Well—she *did* know why she'd said it. It was ruddy obvious Aidan was laying down the ground rules. He didn't want her involved in his personal life. They weren't "a thing."

Which she *knew*! Of *course* she knew... Even though that little-girl, pink-clothes-wearing, dreaming-of-princesses part of her occasionally slipped through the chinks of her armor and let herself imagine...*what if?*

No. There was no "what if?" about it. They'd made a deal, shaken hands and agreed. They were "Colleagues Who Canoodled." Some mighty fine canoodling to boot. The type of canoodling that had sunbeams shooting out of her ears and little sighs of contentment slipping past her lips like a happy, sexy kitten.

Well. A mature kitten. A tigress? Maybe the whole cat analogy was a bad one. At this juncture *any* analogy was a bad one, because she didn't know if she'd just blown the lid off of what they had by—by what, exactly? Daring to dream of something more?

Ali began yanking open the kitchen cupboards on a quest for some zero-zero flour, as per the so-called "super-simple" recipe. She knew she didn't have any, and suddenly the fact that any old flour wouldn't do was a further source of irritation. The contents of her culinary arsenal hadn't really changed from when she'd moved in.

Aidan generally cooked when they were at his place, and they'd have takeaway when they were at hers. And they'd had a fair few away games, too. Away games when, given the chance, she and Aidan would send each other a drink with a wink and a bar mat complete with a hastily scribbled room number. And then... *Bah!*

This whole thing was a disaster. She didn't know why she'd thought she'd be able to rein her heart in and just see Aidan as a bit of edible eye candy when they weren't at work. He was so much more to her. Smart, thoughtful, funny, generous, with about the best head of hair she'd ever run her fingers through in—well, forever. Not to mention the possessor of a bagful of exceedingly sensual moves that had released more than one cry of rapture from her.

Surprise! She'd never known she was a screamer.

She stomped to the kitchen counter and stared at the recipe some more, as if the ingredients would magically fly out of the piece of paper and assemble themselves into a mushroom and mascarpone pizza before her very eyes.

Nope. No good. All she could see was Aidan, giving her his come-hither man winks. *Urrrgh!* They were so *good* together, and as every minute passed it was getting harder and harder to contain her willful heart. She flopped down on the sofa and grabbed the remote. She wasn't really hungry anyway. Perhaps a bit of culture would stem her appetite.

She clicked on the television. Her stomach gurgled.

*Terrific.*

The buzz of her phone had her launching herself across the flat to answer it. Cole was the only one who ever rang "out of hours," and she could do with a dose of her pal right now.

She didn't bother to check the number before answering, "Oh, Lordy, I need to hear your voice!"

"Five hours too long for you, then?"

*Ah.* Not the person she'd expected.

"Sorry, Aidan. I thought you were someone else."

"Oh, so it wasn't *my* voice you were missing?"

*Not just your voice...*

"What's up? How did your training session go?"

"I was just calling to see if you had anything in that pathetic excuse of a kitchen of yours."

*Mind reader.*

"I'm cool."

"I know that, Ali, but I'm guessing you don't have anything for your dinner. How does pizza grab you?"

*Spooky.*

"Mushroom and mascarpone?"

"Just picked it up from the shop. Put your oven on. See you in twenty."

Ali practically skipped to the oven to flick it on to a high heat—they both liked their pizza super-crispy, and it always needed a top-up sear after its journey. And there'd be a huge green salad with peppers and tomatoes tossed in. Not that they were beginning to know each other's preferences or anything. Like a boyfriend and girlfriend would. No…nothing like that at all. Just a couple of colleagues sharing a companionable pizza…

Just two more weeks. She could *do* this.

It was like a litmus test on how mature she was. Sophisticated city girl, coming up to the wilds of the North of England and having a free-spirited love affair…a free-spirited *affair*…with a man who was so ridiculously attractive it was *insane* that he was single.

She needed to keep her cool. There were only

a few more nights when she would be able to be held by him, touch him, make the most of those delicious kisses. Just a teeny-tiny handful of days until the final match and then life would return to normal. Ali would be on her own somewhere out there in the world. A warrior princess, standing her ground. Alone. Just the way she liked it.

"Maybe I should've bought two." Aidan was looking incredulously at Ali. For a slender woman, she could pack it away.

"I went for a run today," she mumbled through her fifth slice of pizza.

"Burning off excess energy?"

"Something like that."

"Ali, I—"

"Yeah?"

She looked at him over the edge of her pizza. She'd been pretty quiet all night. Unusually so. Normally she talked through whatever they watched on television and tonight they'd just watched television. The atmosphere was all wrong. He wanted relaxed and happy Ali back.

"We're all right? The two of us?"

"Of course—what do you mean?" She put on an expression of pure wide-eyed innocence.

"C'mon, Ali. You know what I mean. The 'girlfriend' gaffe. I'm sorry about that."

"Not to worry." She started picking at a piece of mushroom on her pizza, then sent it somersaulting into the empty box between them on the sofa. "It was as much my fault as yours. We work together. And play together. Everything is separate. I get it."

"It's just—"

"Aidan. I *get* it. Could we please not make me feel more mortified than I already do?"

He looked at her in surprise. He'd thought *he* was the one who should be feeling mortified—not her. Lying about his true feelings...? He was most definitely not onto a winner with *that* tack.

"You shouldn't feel badly. I'm the one who stuck my foot in it," Aidan persisted, not entirely sure why he had to get the record straight when in fact that was the last thing he was doing. "I just want to make sure we're good." He reached over and started to trace a finger along her arm in tickly little leaps and hops.

She started laughing and swatted at him. "I thought we weren't going to talk about this anymore?"

"Talk about what?" Shoving everything under the proverbial bed seemed to be working for them. Why change now?

"Precisely." She gave him a mischievous smirk.

Something in the air between them shifted. The awkwardness was replaced with that crackling electricity they shared so well.

"What do you want to do instead?"

Aidan moved his hand up into her hair, tucking little strands back into place. Perfect. He drew his fingers along the thick swatch of hair that trailed down to her collarbone and traced that, too. He'd yet to complete the freckle-count on her décolletage.

"Weeell..." Ali drew out the word as she moved the pizza box to the low table they'd been using as a footrest. "I could think of a couple of things. But I *am* terribly busy, as you can see."

Aidan pulled her onto his lap, no longer interested in the distance between them, however paltry. "C'mere, you."

He drew her to him for a deep kiss, savoring

the taste of her salty lips. He could kiss these lips when they were sweet, salty—whatever. His focus narrowed. He traced his finger along her lower lip as her tongue darted out, ultimately capturing his finger between her teeth and drawing it into her mouth. He sucked in a sharp breath.

Two more weeks. That was all they had. He knew they hadn't really cleared the air between them, but their bodies seemed to have a language of their own, and that would do for now. Ali was on his lap now, her thighs opening wide as she pressed her body to his, her hands holding on to the back of the sofa, her mouth teasing, urging him to commit to something deeper, something more intimate.

He rucked up her shirt and ran his fingertips along her bare back as she dropped kisses and wicked little licks along his neck. Her skin was like silk. He pressed her tightly into him in the vain hope that her scent would be seared into his memory banks. The thought of losing her—not having her with him—threatened his composure. This wasn't enough. Two weeks... Six weeks... It would never be enough. But it was all he had and he was going to be damn sure to make the most of it.

"C'mon." He helped her to her feet and took her hand in his. "I think it's bedtime."

Ali slipped her arm along his waist and gave him a light squeeze.

"I couldn't have put it better myself."

"Doc, we've really got to stop meeting like this."

"Afraid your teammates might start whispering, Mack?" Ali popped a second blood-soaked swab into the medical waste bin. "You're beginning to look a bit like Scarface!"

"That's all part of the plan! The girls love it." Mack gave her a wink.

"Oh, yeah. We just *love* a good ol' roughed up face. The more scars the better!" Ali laughed along with the rookie player. Mack was an up-and-coming star for the North Stars, and was definitely living up to his "Mack Attack" tagline. There wasn't a scrum he didn't want to be a part of.

"Is that why you've gone off Dr. Tate?"

Ali could barely stop her eyes from boinging out of her head at the question, and quickly busied herself with preparing the suture kit. How could she tell him that she and Aidan had shared just about every night together since "That Night" at hot yoga nearly three months ago?

She might as well call their nocturnal liaisons Kama Sutra Class for all the new tiers of love-making she was discovering. Last night had been particularly illuminating. And intense. It was as if their bodies knew there wasn't much time left and saturated every move with greater intensity. Microblasts of heat started detonating inside her as her body relived Aidan's rhythmic movements as she—*ahem*!

She waited to speak until her voice wouldn't sound like a choirboy's. "What makes you say that?"

"Oh, we thought you and Tatey had a thing going on a few weeks back—but obviously even the powerful Harty-attack couldn't tear down the fortress of The Monk's heart."

*Well... That's partly true.*

"Okay—here's the part that's going to hurt." Ali picked up the needle and was just about to take the first stitch when Mack quickly turned away.

"What? You're not afraid of my needlework,

are you?" Ali asked, but she too turned to see what had caught her patient's eye.

"Harty!" Jonesy staggered in, his huge hand covering his face, blood pouring everywhere, "Just got a hands-off." He plopped onto the second examination table in the room and tilted his head back.

"Holy crow, man. Who did *that*?" Mack looked enthralled.

*Little boys. The lot of 'em.*

"Looks more like a hands-*on* to me."

Ali tried her best not to recoil. Ballet stars very rarely had bloody noses, but these guys collected them like badges of honor—and once their noses started spurting they were like unstoppable geysers. At the very least she was developing an incredibly strong stomach.

"Hey, Jonesy. Harty and Tate have broken up."

Ali tutted and tried her best to look nonchalant. Since when had her social life become a discussion point for the team?

"What? No way! I thought you two were cute together. Are we supposed to be like your girlfriends and ask you what happened? Or can we skip that part and let everyone know you're back on the market?" Jonesy sent her a sympathetic yet hopeful look through his bloodied fingers.

"No way! You've both got the wrong idea. There's never been anything going on between us. *Ever*. Never."

Ali lied through her teeth with a slice of genuine horror thrown in. And a splash of admiration for the fact that their "sleeping together" plan had made the atmosphere between them at work seem visibly cooler. Even if it had done the total opposite to her heart. She was still wrestling with that one—big-time.

And as for the couple part? *Hmm...* Aidan had insisted upon regular reminders on that front. A big, fat no-go zone.

Not that she'd protested. They were having fun, weren't they? Just two adults enjoying each other's company. In various stages of undress, mind, but there was no doubting they were enjoying one another. For now. Besides, this sort of explosive attraction never worked out long-term. Short-term suited them, Ali insisted to herself: *a limited edition couple.*

"But when did you break up?" Mack persisted. Since when was he a stickler for details?

"There was never anything to break up *from*! We were never a couple. You boys have clearly suffered too many head injuries."

"What?" Both men protested in unison. Concussions were taken seriously. "Any doubt and you're out" was the coach's motto.

"Enough! The both of you." She wagged a stern finger in each of their directions. Then scowled.

Rugby players needed tough love. It was a world away from the ballet, where cosseting and cajoling worked a treat. She grabbed an ice pack from the well-stocked mini freezer.

"Jonesy, put this on your face. Mack, sit still like a good boy and let me finish these stitches—otherwise you really will look like Scarface. I'm going for a Southern Cross effect. Will that suit?"

"Yes, miss." Mack responded meekly.

"These boys giving you guff?"

"We're all good!" Ali forced herself to reply evenly to the sound of Aidan's voice.

She refused to turn around, focusing fastidiously on the stitches she'd begun. If she was going to continue this highly successful charade, going weak-kneed when their eyes met would be a bit of a giveaway.

"Grand. Lockhart—my office when you're done."

"Yup! Just give me a few minutes with these lugheads and I'll be there."

"Ooh. Harty's in *trouble*!"

Ali couldn't stop herself from swatting at Mack's arm with a bonus glare. It was a bit like wafting tissue paper at a steel beam, but a girl had to try.

"Methinks the lady doth protest too much," Jonesy blurted from beneath his ice cubes.

"Since when do you quote Shakespeare?" Mack guffawed.

"Since I got my degree in English Literature, with a special emphasis on the Elizabethan era. We're not all noodleheads like you, Mack."

"I knew it was Shakespeare," the player retorted.

"Hoo! Color me impressed!" Ali meant it. "Do you have plans to do anything with it, Jonesy? Your degree?"

"I thought I'd go back and get my Masters in teaching once we show the South who dominates the world of rugby. It's not like this gig is going to last forever, and I don't think I'd be any good at coaching. The sidelines aren't my gig."

"Impressive. Not everyone plans for the future. There you go, Mack. All done." Ali tied off the stitches and pressed on a bit of tape. "That should hold your brains in for a while."

She gave him a grin and a "scoot" gesture. Time to sort out Jonesy's nose.

She was really impressed, and strangely proud of this player. It wasn't as if she'd known the man for long, but in the short time she had they had developed a really solid working relationship—heavy with ribbing. She was seriously pleased for him. He was smart to plan for the future. It was something *she'd* have to do, since this little secret liaison thing with Aidan was obviously not going to carry her off into the sunset. Not that she'd ever banked on *that* scenario coming to pass.

Medicine was the only thing she could rely on. But it would be a shame to go all ostrich on herself again—sticking her head back into the medical sandpit of no return. She'd enjoyed setting up the clinic. A lot. And it had eaten up her entire life. That would definitely help keep her mind off Aidan. Maybe she should set up a new one. But where?

Jonesey plonked himself down in front of her, unveiling a blood-slathered face.

America, maybe?

Aidan stared at the whiteboard as if it would help give him some answers.

The only sound in the locker room was the ticking of the clock. He'd never realized how much time elapsed between each second.

He rubbed his eyes, then gave it another inspection.

Nope. No good. That day's skinfold results just weren't going to help him find a way to tell Ali their late-night trysts had to end.

He kicked one of the towels lying on the ground straight up and into the basket on the other side of the room. If only it would be that easy to deal with his father. The man really had unbelievable timing. They had a perfectly amicable long-distance relationship, and now he wanted to come home and show off a new bride...

He let himself sink onto one of the benches,

holding his head in his hands. Unbelievable. Two tiny weeks left with the love of his life and now he had houseguests.

*Tick. Tick.*

Hold on a minute.

*Love of his life?*

No dice. He wouldn't be going down *that* street again. He couldn't. Not after everything life had thrown at him. Five years of holding vigil for a woman—a life—that would never happen. Had it been worth it? Was it worth changing the rulebook now? For this woman who'd whirled into his life, knocked everything sideways and seemed intent on whirling straight back out again?

"Hey!" Ali leaned through the locker room door, giving it a quick knock as she poked her head into the room. "Couldn't find you in your office. Is everything all right?"

"No."

"Oh? It's not Rory, is it? He hasn't been sneaking into the weight room again? I've told him—"

"No."

Ali walked into the room, the door swinging back with into place with a hushed *thwffft*.

*Tick. Tick.*

"Aidan?"

Ali stood in front of him, her brow working on the beginnings of a furrow. *Just look at her.* The most wonderful creature he'd ever known.

*Just two more weeks!* All he'd wanted was to make the most of these two past weeks with her—this amazing woman he was finally beginning to realize he loved. Was that *so* much to ask? Did *everything* he planned have to be swept away before he had a chance to see it through?

Hadn't he paid enough penance for Mary's death?

Couldn't he just have two more weeks before he had to say goodbye?

"I'm presuming this isn't a guessing game and that you are eventually going to tell me what's going on?" Ali nudged his foot with her toe.

"Yes—sorry." He pushed his hands onto his thighs and stood up. He might as well look her in the eye when he did this. He owed her that at least.

"I'm afraid our nocturnal trysts are going to have to end sooner than I thought."

From the look on her face, the news had hit her hard.

"And you thought the locker room was a good place to let me know?"

"Ali, I—I didn't want to draw things out. Now seemed just as bad a time as later."

"Right. Okay."

She gave him a thin smile and looked away. He could hardly blame her.

"That's your fake *I'm cool with it* voice, isn't it?"

"Well, it *is* a bit out of the blue, Aidan. I thought we were—" She broke off to look around the room and ensure they were on their own. "I thought we were enjoying ourselves."

"We were! *Are!*" He raked a hand through his hair. "It's my dad. He's coming to stay."

"Oh!" Her face brightened. "Well, that's not so bad, is it? You can sneak over to mine."

"He's coming with his *new wife*." Aidan tried to weight the words with the depth of meaning they held for him.

"Why are you looking so gloomy? That's great news! Isn't it?"

She peered at him for answers he just didn't have the heart to give. When none were forthcoming, she, too, stared at the skinfold analysis, as if it would offer some code of understanding as to what was going on here.

"You could still come over to mine, couldn't you? It's not like you're sixteen and need your father's permission for a sleepover. Besides..." A bright smile lit up her face. "It would give the newlyweds their own space while they stay with you."

"It's more complicated than that, Ali." Aidan tugged a hand through his hair, fighting an urge to howl at the moon... He looked up at the ceiling. Well...just *howl*. "You and I were meant to be short-term anyway—with my dad here, there would just be too many secrets to worry about keeping. We'd be best just to nip it in the bud now."

A sharp, searing look of pain passed across her eyes as she slowly turned to leave the room. If he could've pulled her into his arms and told her everything was going to be all right he would've. The churning in his gut told him he owed her more than he was giving her—and the best but most painful way to do that was to let her go.

"Ali, I—"

"Please don't, Aidan. Really. I get it. If you

don't mind, I think I'll just get back to work in lieu of you rubbing some more salt into my wounds."

"This was hardly what I wanted, Ali. I just received my father's email. I'm still reeling myself."

"From *what*, exactly, Aidan? A visit from your *dad*?" She threw her hands up in bewilderment. "That sounds like a *nice* thing to me. The money I wouldn't give to have my mum back for a just a few hours, let alone a proper visit… You're lucky to have him."

"It's not—*aaarghhh*! It's not the same."

"Right."

Ali squared herself up to him, arms crossed firmly over her chest. He had to give it to her: she wasn't one to give up ground lightly.

"What's so different about your dad that makes having him alive and wanting to visit his son with his new wife so awful?"

"Long story."

She glanced at her watch. "I've got until the next groin injury or bleeding beak comes stumbling in that door. Could be minutes. Could be hours." She pointed at the bench. "Sit. Speak. If you're going to rob me of my final days of the best booty calls I've ever had, I deserve an explanation."

Aidan couldn't help himself. He had to laugh. This woman had mettle. It was going to eat him alive that their final few days together would be relegated to pitch-side.

"Spill it, Tate." She sat down on the bench beside him, giving him a poke in the arm for good measure.

And he did. He told her about his mother leaving when he was a teen. How his father had been absolutely destroyed by her departure. He told her how he'd had to take over making meals, cleaning the house, making sure his father—a successful sportswriter—got to work, went to games, took showers, turned in his stories on time so he would get paid. How his teenaged girlfriend had become his helpmeet. Had risen to the occasion. How she'd been there for him and his father—particularly his father—when they had needed it, and—

"And...?" Ali asked quietly.

"And when I went to med school, she took over for me. You know—checking in on him, making sure he didn't get scurvy or anything. She just looked after him up until he moved to the West Indies for work."

Ali shot him a questioning look.

"He needed to move on. And he did. Successfully. I thought it was time for me to take the next step with my girlfriend, so we went away to the Pacific Islands—"

Ali's breath froze in her chest. *The tropical storm. The charity work.* Everything fell into place with a riotous clash in her heart. Aidan was caught. Caught in the thick nets of the past. And he couldn't see his way to break free.

She tipped her head so she could see what was happening in Aidan's eyes. They normally sparked with life. She'd never seen him this down.

Her stomach sank. Aidan's words were really beginning to sink in now. It was over. His father was too close a link to the past he had never recovered from. No wonder he compartmentalized everything so much. It made his life bearable.

Aidan stared straight ahead and continued to speak. "I was busy being pragmatic. Sensible. Life with my dad had taught me to hold every card I had tight to my chest. He'd already had a series of girlfriends by that point, and I'd learned better than to expect to see any of them for more than a few weeks or months before a new one would turn up."

The words began pouring out of him. Ali pressed her fingers to her lips, eyes widening as he spoke. She knew what was coming.

"I thought it would be prudent to wait a few days into our holiday before I proposed. You know—make sure we could relax together as well as we worked together."

"And did you?"

Ali knew she shouldn't be jealous, but a teensy bit of her was envious of the woman who had known a younger Aidan. An Aidan who would've looked at the world through less jaded eyes. The more time she spent with him, the more she wanted. And now he was spelling it out in triplicate why it was all over between them.

She scuffed at the locker room floor with the toe of her shoe. Aidan wasn't the only one who thought life was harsh.

"We were one of those steady couples. It had always been…" His eyes wandered around the locker room as if hunting for the best word "*Easy.*

It had always just been easy with her. I liked her. She liked me. No wild fireworks like—" He tipped his head in her direction with a wry smile playing along his lips.

His face was wreathed in such unbearable sadness it nearly broke Ali's heart. She wanted to touch him. Hold him. She knew how awful it was to lose someone. And she also knew there was nothing she could say to make it better. She wished for her mother to be back every day of her life, and only just managed to fill the void with medicine. It seemed as though Aidan had done the same thing for different reasons.

She watched as his dark eyes locked on the wall across from him. His voice took on a wrenchingly hollow tone.

"The tropical storm hit in the morning. I was up on the balcony of our room, reading, and she'd gone out snorkeling with a couple we had met the night before. I had this paper I wanted to write and some reading to finish up—I thought I'd save the proposal for the evening. You know—the romance of moonlight and all that claptrap."

Ali clapped her fingers to her mouth. *How awful.* Her heart ached for him.

"Did you ever see her again?"

Ali didn't know why, but if she'd been in the same situation she would have wanted to see the body, to say goodbye properly. She'd been able to say farewell to her mother before she'd passed. The painful heartbreak of those moments haunted her to this day, but at least she had had them. She had no doubt of the love her mother had for her—and she knew her mother had died with the knowledge that her daughter would honor her forever.

"No. I stayed on for a few months, helping with the volunteer medical corps, but after a while it was obvious it was a futile search. They'd been snorkeling out on a boat beyond the cluster of islands where we'd been staying. The whole thing was a nightmare. An absolute living nightmare."

She couldn't even begin to imagine. And for the first time in a long time felt at an utter loss for words. What did you say to someone who had experienced something like that? How did you pick the words that could even begin to explain how deeply you felt for their loss? You tried your best...

"And yet you still watch zombie films?"

Aidan turned to her as her face snapped into a horrified *oops* expression.

"Sorry—that was about the least sensitive thing I could've said."

"No." He patted her leg as he rose from the bench with a sad smile. "The one thing I can always count on when I spend time with you is to be cheered up." He added, "Truly," when she raised a dubious eyebrow. "Thanks, Ali. I mean it. Having you around makes the world a nicer place."

Ali felt cemented to the bench as she watched Aidan push through the swinging doors of the locker room toward the corridor where his office lay.

The world hadn't really given him much of a break, had it? No wonder he preferred to keep her at arm's length. A heartbroken father? A young love that never had a chance to see itself through? It couldn't have been that long ago... Maybe five...six years? If time had done to him what it had done to her after her mum died, he would hardly have noticed it flashing by.

She pressed herself up from the bench, wondering what had broken his heart more—the loss of his girlfriend or never knowing what would have happened if he had proposed. Maybe the two were so interwoven it was impossible to tell.

She pushed out of the locker room and headed toward her own office. She could always count on work to be there for her. But this time she should learn from the past—make progress, as Aidan had said his father eventually had. She would work hard—but be realistic. Not push life to the wayside as she had before.

Losing her booty calls with Aidan was definitely going to be a tough ask, but she knew in her heart she would do anything to see that bright spark of life in his eyes again—even if it meant backing off. For good.

# CHAPTER EIGHT

"CAN YOU SEE who it is?" Ali went onto her tip-toes, as if that would help her see through the thick wall of uniforms surrounding a player on the ground.

The referee looked to their side of the pitch and made a signal.

"One of ours. Head injury. I'll take it," Aidan replied grimly as he grabbed his bag and began to jog toward the huddle of players.

Grim was the only tone he'd been using lately, and work was the only thing that was helping him get through the day. Not that he wished his players ill—but focusing on them was a damn sight easier than thinking about his father's impending arrival. It had churned up just about every bit of history he'd worked so hard to tamp down into the past.

And being away from Ali hadn't brought the balm of Alone Time he'd thought it would.

The only thing he'd achieved was a first-class foul mood.

A couple of nights on his own had seemed sensible—pragmatic. Time to rebuild the protective barrier around his heart. If his father fell to pieces again he wasn't so sure how strong a support system he would be. Not now. No one to lean on. No one to just—*be there*.

The emptiness of the past forty-eight hours had only drilled into him how much a part of his life Ali had become. Instead of feeling empowered by the absence of their entanglement all he felt was an overwhelming desire to tell Ali more. Hash out his past and untangle the weave of his history to create something new. Something that made him feel ridiculously alive—as he had ever since he'd met her. This whole "nipping it in the bud" idea was beginning to look like a contender for Stupidest Idea Ever.

"Doc, it's Chris." One of the players opened a gap in the huddle around the North Stars player to let him in.

"That's a nice egg you're growing on your pate, Chris."

"Thanks, Doc. Anything for some sympathy."

He remained flat on the ground despite his stab at humor.

"That'd be about right. Do you know what half we're in?"

"Don't be ridiculous. We're not playing in a match. This is a practice."

"Can you take your hands away from your head for a minute? I need you to focus on my finger." He held his index finger up and began a slow arc across Chris's eyeline.

"Don't take the mick, Doc. You've got two fingers up there. I know a trick question when I see one. I mean two..."

"Right!" Aidan pushed himself up decisively. "Nice and easy, boys. Can you help Chris up?"

"I'm perfectly fine to— *Whoooooahhh*!" Chris lurched up and then clonked back down to the ground. "I. Want. To. Play." He spoke progressively more and more slowly.

"Lads?" Aidan signaled to two of the players to lift him up.

It was definitely a concussion. How severe it was remained to be seen. For now he just needed to get Chris off of the field and into the stadium's clinic. The stretcher team was right behind him if he needed more help, and there was an ambulance standing by if he was concerned about internal bleeding.

He tucked his shoulder underneath one of Chris's lumberjack-sized arms and began a slow walk off the field, to the supportive cheers of the fans.

"Easy, there, Chris. I've gotcha."

"Do you need a hand bringing him down the tunnel?" Ali rushed to help as they reached the edge of the field.

"No. You need to stay here!" Aidan snapped.

"No need to bite Harty's head off, Doc. It's obvious the woman just wanted a chance to put her arms around me," Chris joked through his very obvious pain.

"Dr. Tate's right." Ali gave the player's arm a pat. "You just look after yourself and do as you're told."

"Yes, miss." Chris threw her a grin as a stony-faced Aidan led him down the tunnel toward the medical room.

Ali didn't think Aidan had smiled once since he'd told her the news of his father's arrival, and her heart ached for him. She was trying her best to give him room to breathe, but being at this away game had meant an enforced coach ride together because the coach had wanted to talk through some of their players' injuries, and the hotel had put their rooms adjacent to the others. She had actually laughed out loud when she'd gone to her room to drop her tote and had seen it had one of those connecting doors that would've allowed her to slip into his room unnoticed. If it weren't locked tight.

Ha-bloody-ha! Wasn't life sweet?

She went back to the bench as play recommenced and joined Rory, who insisted on watching all of the games from the sidelines in full uniform despite still being on the mend.

"You don't leave your teammates in the lurch just because you're hurtin', Harty," he'd quipped.

She'd nearly burst into tears at the words. It was physically painful not to be there for Aidan when he was so obviously hurting. But she knew well enough when someone needed to go through something on their own. She'd gone through her own dark tunnel and... Was she out of it? At the very least she knew she could see the light.

She pressed her fingernails into her palms and

threw a forlorn look in the direction of the medical room. No sign of Aidan. Probably just as well. What had seemed a short two weeks when they had been "together" had suddenly turned into an endless stretch of seconds, minutes and hours that would never end. They were down to eight days now. One hundred and ninety-two more hours. Fewer if she could escape to the train station right after the final match. She thought steering clear of airports would be a wise move.

"So, Harty. You think I'll be ready for the final?" Rory gave her a good-natured elbow in the ribs.

"Let's see what Mr. X-ray Machine has to say when we get back tomorrow, okay? How much training have you been doing?"

"Same as the other lads, minus any weights. Well, *heavy* weights. I've even been back to that hot yoga you made us all do a few weeks back. It's good, that."

Ali smiled at the memory and just as quickly felt it fade. That had been the night she and Aidan had been honest with one another and set the world alight. Well, *her* world, anyway. So much for honesty being the best policy...

"Sounds good, Rory. As long as you're listening to your body and playing it safe I don't see any reason why we won't see you out there."

"Ace. Thanks, Doc."

"Don't take that as a sure thing!" she warned, knowing she was the one who needed to be taking her own advice.

If only her heart—not to mention her body—would stop telling her how much she wanted Aidan, life would be a whole lot easier.

"Hey, Harty!"

One of the players called her from the entrance to the hotel bar—the only quiet spot she'd been able to find where the internet worked.

"You joining us for dinner? We've found a ripper of a steakhouse—coach approves!"

"Ooh, you risk-takers! Skinfold tests tomorrow! Beware the banoffee pie!" she teased, then waved away his invitation. "I'm going to have a quiet one, I think. See you in the morning."

"You bet."

He disappeared around the corner and she stared at her laptop, willing it to offer her some guidance. Who could she email for some advice?

The cursor blinked at her, as if daring her to type in someone's name. She really needed a friend, and the one she really needed—wanted—right now was a closed book.

That telltale stinging began in her nose and it took real effort to swallow down the threat of tears. She wasn't much of a crier, but the past few days had seen her teetering on the brink of weeping more than once.

It didn't take a brain surgeon—or in this case a highly trained doctor—to figure out what the problem was. One six-foot-something, black-haired, chestnut-eyed problem was her problem. She was in love with Aidan, and he couldn't be making it clearer that a future together was about as likely as Ali getting up in her toe shoes again.

She closed down the email program. She'd dealt with that part of her life. Not dancing again. She loved medicine and, whilst dancing with the best would've been amazing, she wouldn't change her life one bit.

Or would she? Would she reel back the past few months? The hours of scorching passion she'd spent with Aidan? The days of working with him, growing and learning together?

The part of her that could look at the situation with clinical accuracy was beyond reach. Then again, the truth boiled down to something very simple: she wanted Aidan in her life and that wasn't an option—so she was just going to have to get a grip.

"For the lady." The bartender appeared in front of her with a cocktail.

A Cosmopolitan.

Her heart rate instantly accelerated and she looked to the other end of the bar. There he was, as gorgeous as the first day she'd laid eyes on him—Aidan Tate.

"May I join you?"

"Aren't you eating with the team?"

"Doesn't look like it, does it?" He walked over minus an invitation.

"No need to raise your hackles—it was only a question."

Ali pressed her lips together tightly. Maybe she should just call Cole at En Pointe and say she needed her old life back. The cold-blooded one. Immediately.

Eight days suddenly seemed like an eternity.

"I wasn't—" Aidan began sharply, then stopped

himself with an equally abrupt change of demeanor. "When I saw you in here it just reminded me..." He didn't bother finishing.

"I know," Ali replied softly, not trusting herself to touch him despite the fact that his hand was resting just within temptation's reach. Three days ago she would have. But now wasn't then. "It reminded me, too."

She let her finger trace up the slender stem of the cocktail glass, already beading with condensation. She'd never believed it was possible to actually feel your heart breaking until this very moment.

"Well, aren't *we* the happy couple?" Aidan lifted his glass with a sad smile. "Cheers."

Ali raised her cocktail and clinked glasses with him. As she brought the glass to her lips the scent of the alcohol in the drink went straight to her gut. It was all she could do to keep her tummy in check as intense waves of nausea began to build within her.

"I'm sorry, Aidan. Will you excuse me?"

"No time for a drink with a colleague?"

It was unbearable to see the disappointment in

his face. She felt it too. But she had to get out of there—and fast.

"It's not that. Sorry... I'm just not feeling very well."

"Anything I can do?" He reached toward her and she pulled away, tucking her laptop in front of her chest as if it would protect her heart from any more pain.

*Oh, blimey.* She really wasn't feeling well at all.

"No, no. I'll be all right. Sorry about the drink."

She winced as she said the words, but knew time wasn't on her side. If she didn't get to her room... *Too late.* Ali grabbed hold of the doorframe to the bar and, despite her best efforts, returned her lunch to the world.

*Talk about mortifying!*

"Ali! Are you all right?"

"What do you think?" She didn't have the wherewithal to pull her elbow away from Aidan's supportive hold.

"Don't worry, madam. We'll get it cleaned up for you." The bartender had arrived with several cloths and handed her a dampened serviette. "Would you like me to call a doctor?"

"I *am* a doctor."

"*I* am a doctor." Aidan's voice was stronger than hers.

She glared at him, as if that would help take away the relief she felt that he was there by her side. But having him as her support system wasn't her destiny.

"I'd just like to go to my room, if that's all right."

"I'll walk you there."

"*No.*" She gritted her teeth together, then forced herself to offer Aidan a polite smile. They were in public, after all. "Thank you."

"Don't be ridiculous. My room is next to yours anyway, so it's not like it's out of my way."

"Would you like your drinks sent to your room? Rooms...?" the bartender asked, obviously unsure how to wrap up a situation of this nature.

"No!" They each answered definitively.

"Right you are, then. I'll just call Housekeeping." He turned away on his heel, obviously annoyed at their collective terseness.

Aidan started to giggle first. Ali couldn't help but join him. By the time they hit the elevator and its doors had firmly shut they were in the throes of a full-on belly laugh.

It felt nice. To be laughing with Aidan. She chanced a glance up at him and saw he felt the same thing. It would've been so easy to step right back into his arms, feel the warmth of his chest. Nestle into that perfect little spot that made it so easy for him to rest his cheek on her head while she listened to his heartbeat.

The elevator lurched to a halt, instantly reminding Ali of why they were headed to their rooms in the first place. Another wave of nausea was threatening to defeat her ability to retain control over her stomach. What on earth was going on? She hadn't eaten anything suspect for lunch. It couldn't be food poisoning.

"Are you all right? You look awfully pale."

"I'll be fine. I think a good lie-down is all I need."

Ali slipped her key into the door and pushed it open before turning to face Aidan. *C'mon, girl, be nice. He's trying to help.*

"Maybe this is the other team's attempt to take us all out with food poisoning!"

"Great hypothesis—except you're the only one being sick."

"It's a working theory. I'm willing to explore more options."

Aidan looked down at her with an expression that was anything but amused. "I'm right next door if you need anything."

"I'll be fine."

She tucked herself behind the door, making it clear she was going solo. He was too close. And, no matter how much she could do with an Aidan-shaped pillow in bed, right now she needed him elsewhere. *Now.*

"Honestly." She gave him what she hoped looked like a nonchalant smile. "I'll be fine."

Two hours later, "fine" was the last thing Ali felt. She'd forced herself to lie in bed after Aidan had left and had gone through a medical check-list as to what could have caused her to be sick so suddenly.

One panicked trip to a nearby chemists later and feeling "fine" was something she knew would be unbelievably hard to come by.

Excited, confused, terrified...

Those she could do.

She stared at the plastic stick in her hand again

as if it might have been lying to her. Then she stared at the other one.

Nope. Two stripes on each, and she hadn't got a concussion.

She was pregnant.

And the only man who could be the father was one very thin wall away.

# CHAPTER NINE

AIDAN STOOD IN the airport Arrivals hall, a stream of speeches already going through his head. None of them were particularly fair. His father hadn't been the bad guy in his first marriage, and if he'd found happiness at long last the only thing Aidan should be feeling was happiness.

His dad was an amazing guy. Social, laser-smart, professionally still at the fore of his game. He was a great catch. And yet he couldn't help but think, *Why him and not me?*

It wasn't jealousy. It was pure frustration that his dad had managed to move beyond his unhappy past and *he* hadn't. He just hadn't reconciled a way to move forward after Mary had died.

Ah! There he was. Richard Tate. Definitely a contender for the "silver-haired fox" category. He'd recognize that head of hair anywhere and—

*Oh, my word.*

*Is that...?*

*Did he...?*

Aidan didn't know whether to be happy or mystified at the strangeness of humankind. It appeared, from the beaming faces of the happy couple, that his father had gone and married his divorce lawyer. How on earth...?

"Hello, son!"

"Hey, Dad. And it's Marianne, isn't it?"

"Well, I'm not going to start making you call me 'Mother,' if that's what you're worried about."

Marianne gave him a warm smile and much to his amazement he felt himself returning it. He was *genuinely* happy for his father. After the tightness in his heart these past few days it was a relief to let the clamps loosen—if only just a bit.

"I take it you approve?" His father gave him a knowing look.

"Father! What on earth do you mean?" Aidan took charge of their luggage trolley and began guiding them toward the car park, a big grin playing on his lips. "I approve of *all* your wise decisions."

"Oh, don't be coy with me, son." He made an unsuccessful attempt to commandeer the luggage trolley and then opted to swing an arm over his wife's shoulders instead. "I think you'll be happy to know I have finally—after some rather extensive and heavily faulty experimentation—found 'The One.'"

Aidan had to work hard not to give him a dubious look.

Marianne gave a happy laugh at her new husband's declaration of love and smiled knowingly at Aidan. "At least you can be sure if it doesn't work out I know how to *really* put the screws in when it comes to the divorce."

The couple began to absolutely crease themselves with laughter, as if she'd just said the funniest thing in the entire world. Divorce didn't seem on the immediate horizon from the looks of things.

Aidan shook his head and smiled. You could've knocked him over with a feather right now. What was it they said? There was nowt so queer as folk...

Too bad life hadn't been as generous to him and Ali. His lips settled into a straight line. They'd hardly exchanged a word since they'd left that away game, and he could hardly blame her.

What was he doing, anyway? Keeping her at arm's length for exactly *what* benefit? Closing down what had been a perfect fit? She was smart, sexy as hell and she had no quarrel with standing up to him—there was definitely a bit of "like father, like son" in *that* department. Was he carving his own history into something he had predetermined it to be? An unhappy one?

Aidan began to unload their luggage into the trunk of his car as Marianne and his father play-bickered over who would get the front seat. They looked happy. Genuinely happy. Which was exactly how he felt when he was with Ali. Excepting these past torturous seventy-two hours, when he'd most likely ruined any chance of getting back into her good books.

He hoped she was all right. Leaving her on her own after she had been unwell at the hotel hadn't sat right—but he was trying to respect her wishes. It was the least he could do after unceremoniously dumping her. Because that was what he'd done. Just like he'd done to every other woman he'd dated. Only this time it had been different. This time he hadn't meant a single word. Seeing his father so happy, so content, was a glaring confirmation that he'd done the wrong thing when it came to Ali.

And the chances of fixing it? Making things right with her?

An image of her closing the door in his face flickered through his mind's eye.

*Nil.*

She'd accepted the terms of their deal. And he didn't blame her. She would think herself a fool to fly back into the arms of a man who played hot and cold. Unless he were to tell her that he loved her.

The thought unsettled him. He didn't do love. He did casual.

This was all just sentiment, right? He was letting surprise at his father's choice of bride soften his resolve. Sure, they were happy *now*—but that was how relationships were in the beginning. All giggly and fun in the first few months.

Even as the words flowed through his mind they felt wrong. He'd known about Ali from the moment he'd laid eyes on her. Getting to know her had only cemented in stone what he hadn't been brave enough to put into words then: he loved her. Heart and soul.

He raked a hand through his hair and slammed the lid of the trunk down with a satisfying clang. He'd blown it with Ali and it was just as well. He'd just have to find a way to live with the consequences.

"Son! You've got human beings in the car here!" His father stuck his head out the window. "What gives?"

"Sorry, Dad... Marianne. Forgot about your old jangling bones!" he joked, not feeling the remotest bit cheery. "Just a bit distracted by work." He slipped into the car and started the engine.

"Anything we can do to help?" Marianne asked from the back seat.

*Apart from winning back the heart of the woman I love and proving true love can last? No. Not really.*

"How about you magically heal our flanker's clavicle and pray for no more groin injuries?"

Marianne made a *youch* face in the rearview mirror.

"What about we take you out to dinner tonight after work, son? Then you won't have to worry about cooking or anything.

"Sounds good, Dad."

And for the first time in a very, very long time a night with his father and his new wife sounded like something he would genuinely look forward to.

Ali looked up from her desk at the sound of Aidan's knock on her office doorframe. Her tummy did a flip as their eyes caught. Was it the baby or her who was reacting to seeing him? Surely the baby was too small? And it wasn't as if she was unaware of the effect Aidan had on her.

As if to press the point, her fingers began to tingle. So she sat on them. "How'd it go at the airport?"

"Good! They're sleeping off their jetlag and we're meeting up for dinner later. But it went well! She's really nice."

"You look surprised."

"It seems my father has gone and done something wise."

Aidan leaned against the doorframe, all lean-sexy-man-style. Oh, she *really* wished he wouldn't do that. This was what he would do in the mornings when he brought her coffee. Stand in the doorframe and watch her for a moment, before coming into the room and giving her a long, slow kiss.

Her hand snuck out from under her leg and began to trace her lips. She couldn't help it. They were missing his touch. *All of her* was missing his touch.

Didn't he have work to do? As long as he was out of sight she'd have more time to think up the right combination of words to tell him he was going to be a father. He had a right to know. Then she'd tell him he didn't have to worry. That she and the baby would be all right on their own.

She blinked up at Aidan and realized he was looking at her expectantly. Was she meant to have said something?

"Sorry—what was that?"

"My father..."

Aidan peered at her curiously. She guessed she hadn't hidden the thoughts racing round her mind all that well.

"He's married quite a wonderful woman."

"That's great!" Ali enthused, using every bit of strength she had to maintain a bright smile.

Now what? Should she say, *Give them my best, and while you're at it you may as well let them know they're going to be grandparents in about seven months' time!*

"Yeah. You should meet her. You'd like her."

"Sure. Absolutely! That'd be great!"

*Lordy.* She sounded like a wind-up fairy on a sugar high.

"Um…" She pointed at the paperwork on her desk. "I've just got to go through these stats. Shall we catch up later?"

"No problem."

Aidan gave her a sideways glance. One that told her in an instant that he knew something was up but wasn't going to push it. For which she was grateful. She still needed time. Time to formulate a Big Picture plan before dropping her bombshell.

Her little, tiny, baby-shaped bombshell.

Ali had to face facts. There were only so many cotton buds a person could fit into the plastic container she was twirling round and round, trying to divine a small spot for just one more teeny-tiny bud. Was that so much to ask? A bit more room to make things fit? Ditto cotton swabs, knee braces, ankle braces, crepe bandages, sock tape, grip enhancers and zinc oxide tapes. Her run bag was officially full to bursting.

She sat back in her chair with a huff.

She had to face facts. No amount of tidying was going to change the reality that she still hadn't told Aidan she was pregnant with his baby. And that instead of feeling absolutely horrified she felt abuzz with a myriad of sensations.

The sensation she felt most of all was *happy*. Really, truly, fire-burning-in-her-belly happy. Not a literal fire, of course, because that would hurt the baby, and already—just one attack of nausea and a few early nights in—she felt a fierce need to protect the microscopic little creature.

By her estimation the baby would be eight weeks, one day and—she glanced up at the wall clock—thirteen or so hours old. Not that she'd been racking her brains trying to figure out the moment of conception or anything. There had been that "incident" with a condom on the first night they'd shared, so it looked as if she was living proof that nothing was foolproof.

It wasn't too strange that she'd missed the signs. She'd had a period after "The Great Airport Liaison," so hadn't thought twice about the protection malfunction.

Ali stared at the tip of the cotton bud. Was this how big it was? The baby? A little four-and-a-half-millimeter being, busy developing a circulatory system, buds for arms and legs, all of its teeny-tiny internal organs taking shape.

If she was eight weeks along it would already be forming itsy-bitsy ears, eyes, and a little-bitty upper lip. One that, when it was fully developed and she was holding their—*her*—baby in her arms, she would trace with her finger as if it was the most amazing thing in the world. Which it was, considering she was using all sorts of gooey baby talk in her head.

She was a *scientist*, for heaven's sake. Someone who always retained her cool.

A memory of raking her nails down Aidan's back as he teased first his fingers and then his—*stop*!

*Almost* always retained her cool.

When she hadn't had her period last month she'd just written it off to a combination of adrenaline, a new level of fitness because she'd been working out so much and…well…honestly…?

Who wanted a monthly visitor when you were having such a great time mattress-testing? Besides, her periods had never been regular.

She'd been too busy sliding down rainbows and twirling round pots of gold, thinking how happy she was with her life up here. A dreamy little life, way up here on Cloud Nine. Until Aidan had yanked away the fluffy cloud and abruptly plonked her back down to planet earth.

*Jerk.*

*Perfectly perfect jerk.*

How on earth was she going to tell him? It ate at her heart that he couldn't see beyond his past, but that was the way their cookie crumbled. She'd certainly let her lack of a future in dance maul her soul for a while. She understood how disappointment could eat away at you.

Apart from which, if the baby *had* been conceived on that night at the airport there really would have been every chance she'd never have seen him again. Two people put together by a heavy snowfall to make a baby. *Her* baby. If she thought of it that way—took away the Aidan she had fallen in love with—it was easier to bear. By a smidge.

So... She drew in a deep breath. This was how it would be: Ali and her very own little baby, creating a brand-new family. The Lockhart Duo! Just like she and her mother had been. She'd never dreamed of being anything but on her own after her mother died—so this was good. Just different than what she'd planned.

Ali leaned back in her chair, using her toes to push herself back and forth. She'd known for about five days and seventeen hours and she wasn't sure the news had sunk in with her— let alone given her enough time to calmly tell Aidan he was going to be a father. Each time she'd opened her mouth to say something there had either been an interruption or she'd lost the courage.

*She had to tell him.* At the very least it was his right to know. Especially since she was going to see this through. She was going to have the baby.

As the thought paraded through her brain a whole new set of nerves sent a fresh course of adrenaline through her. She'd have to go to yoga tonight after work—not hot yoga...that wouldn't be good for the baby. But yoga—the calming sort—was a must if she was ever going to rein in her composure enough to tell Aidan. Which she would. When she found the right time. *If* she found the right time.

*Oh, golly, gosh—and a Moses basket to boot!*

She was simply going to *have* to find a time.

She tried to picture what his face would look like after she told him—said the words *We're having a baby.* Or *I'm having a baby.* Maybe that would be better. No. Then it might sound like someone else could've been in the picture. *As if.*

*There is a baby.*

No. Too scientific. And vague.

*Remember at the airport, when we were pretending we didn't care it was Valentine's Day, decided to skip dinner and went straight to the great sex part? We ate ice cream after. Choc chip mint. With fudge sauce. Which I licked off your—*

No. Inappropriate for a baby-reveal.

Then again... Maybe it hadn't been that night after all. It could have been that night they'd each got rug burns. Or...

*Aaaaaargh! No, no, no, no, no, noooooooooo!*

She plonked her head down on her desk with a clonk. Her speech needed work.

"Lockhart?" Coach Stone gave the doorframe of her office a quick knock before entering. "You all right to do the skinfolds this morning? Tate's off doing X-rays with Rory."

"Absolutely." She smiled and grabbed her caliper. "Be there in a mo."

Work. The perfect distraction. It had helped her get through tough times before. But this time it was going to be much harder to put the blinkers on and block out the obvious. She was in love with Aidan Tate and she was going to have his baby—and those weren't things Aidan wanted in his life: a relationship, a baby. A family. The sooner she got that through her thick skull, the better.

She pushed into the locker room and as the fug of sweaty man scent, dirty towels, smelly rugby cleats and fifteen different varieties of deodorant hit her she found herself trying to knock back another powerful wave of nausea.

"You all right, Harty?" one of the players asked as she barely stopped herself from swooning at the sensation. "You're looking a bit green around the gills."

"Did you guys run out of shower gel or something?" She cracked a smile but had to hold on to the doorframe to help her collect herself before entering the locker room. It had never seemed this rank before. What had these guys been *doing* all morning?

"You didn't go and get yourself pregnant at one of our away games, did you, Harty?"

Her stomach turned again. "Ha-ha. Very funny." She forced herself to let go of the doorframe.

*Must remember to mouth-breathe.* That should just about get her through the next half hour in here.

"Come on, Mack. You're up first, fatty!" She opened the calipers in an evil scientist clamping motion and left the doorway. She could do this.

As she tried to stride into the center of the room a huge waft of tropical heat hit her when one of the players came out of the steam room. Unsteadiness began to work its way through her, as if she were a huge bobble woman. The players and the lockers began to spin around her. She could see but not hear Mack as he approached her, arms outstretched, and then—darkness.

Aidan gave the coach an incredulous look. Ali? *His* Ali had fainted?

"I don't know what happened, Aidan. She just came into the locker room to do the caliper tests, and next thing you know was out like a light in Mack's arms. One of the boys found some salts and she was back up at work as if nothing had happened a few minutes later, but it was strange."

"What? She fainted because Mack was holding her?" That didn't sound like Ali—and he didn't like the idea of her being in another man's arms.

"No, no. She fainted and he caught her because he was on his way to her to get his skinfold test." Coach Stone gave him a sideways glance. "What does it matter, anyway? Point is, Lockhart fainted for no apparent reason, and you need her on top form tomorrow for the final or you need to get someone new in here. *Stat.* Are we clear?"

"Absolutely, Coach. I'll go speak with her."

"You do that. We need absolutely no diversions tomorrow."

The coach was serious. The team had done

incredibly well this season, and he had all but cleared a prime spot in the display cabinets of the North Stars' trophy room. They were all in the same place—on the same mission. Fainting doctors weren't really a goer at this point.

Strange, though. When he'd last seen Ali she'd been perfectly... No, she hadn't. She'd been distracted. *Very* distracted. Maybe she had some sort of bug. There was always something going around this time of year as the seasons shifted. If that was the case he didn't want her anywhere near the team. It wasn't how he'd been hoping to see out the last day he had with her—but if he had to ban her from the game, he would. He'd chosen work and he needed to stay true to that.

Aidan pushed out of the locker room's double doors and headed for her office. They'd barely spoken since his father had arrived. Everything between them was the opposite of how he'd imagined their final days together would be. If he had been a wall-puncher his apartment would have been riddled with holes.

This was just the sort of scenario he should've pictured before he'd let himself get carried away with—with *what*, exactly? Falling in love with

Ali Lockhart? That was about the size of it. He just didn't know how to picture it, though. Never had. Marriage to the girl of his dreams and living happily ever...? Didn't he give himself an annual reminder as to why that was *never* going to happen?

He stuck his head round Ali's office door. She was wholly engrossed in finishing up some paperwork and he stole the few moments to soak her in. Ebony hair falling down her back and over her shoulder in thick waves. Long fingers playing at her lips while she chose what to write on the forms. He narrowed his focus to the pads of her fingers, tip-tapping along her lips—lips he knew he could never tire of kissing.

He straightened and abruptly cleared his throat. This sort of mooning wasn't going to get him anywhere.

"Hey, there." Ali turned round in her chair, eyebrows slightly raised in expectation.

"Mind if I come in?"

"Please." Ali indicated a chair—not the one closest to her desk, he noticed. Fair enough. It wasn't as if he'd been unleashing a welcoming parade of late.

"Coach wanted me to check on how you were feeling."

She tilted her head to the side, as if she were considering what to say, then gave a dry laugh. "I'm fine." She looked him in the eye. "Anything else?"

"Are you sure? You don't think you've got a bug or something? I heard about the fainting."

Ali pressed her lips together. Hard. Then let them scrape past her teeth before allowing herself to answer. She'd left it too long to tell Aidan now. The day before the final. Destroying his focus when he needed it most Was not really the plan of action she'd been going for. She would tell him directly after the final. And then she'd leave.

"I'm fine, Aidan. Just putting together the team's final set of health stats before the big day."

He nodded, rubbed his hands along his thighs and gave his hands a clap, as if he was gearing up to saying something big. "Good, good. Anything interesting?"

*Uh... I'm pregnant with your baby.*

*Out loud, voice—please! Otherwise Aidan's going to keep hovering, and the longer he stands here the more you're going to want to slip into his arms and be held for one lovely, long, Aidan-scented last time before you have to say goodbye.*

"Mack seems to have the most consistently low resting heart rate of the lot," she mustered, in her bright-as-a-bluebird voice. "And..." She ran her finger along the chart she was currently working on. "Looks like Jonesey wins on the skinfold test—although they're all really in peak condition. I would say there's not much more than a hair's breadth between them."

"Great. As well they should be. Coach has been working them hard." Aidan moved to the doorway but didn't seem to be making much of an effort to actually leave the room, which would've been the ideal outcome.

"That he has!" Ali smiled at him, hoping her expression said *We're done now.* Her veneer of cheer was about to crack, so his departure would be good.

"You wouldn't...?" Aidan's voice trailed off.

*For the sweet love of an ending! Spit it out, man! There are not so many hours left in this day, and that means there are fewer than twenty-four more before you hear you're going to be a father.*

"Wouldn't *what*, Aidan?" Ali was finding it hard to mask her exasperation.

"You wouldn't like to come out to dinner with me tonight? To meet my dad and his wife," he added hastily.

*Unexpected.*

He gave her one of those pretty-please smiles of his that she found virtually impossible to resist.

"There's a lot to do before tomorrow..." she stalled.

"C'mon Ali. You've got to eat."

Aidan sat down in the chair next to her desk and took her hand in his. Her nerve endings shot to attention and it was all she could do not to climb into his lap, wrap her arms around his neck and tell him everything.

"Help me out here."

"What? By having dinner with your dad and your new *stepmum*?"

She knew the word would rankle. Which was precisely why she'd said it. He pulled his hand away from hers—just as she'd predicted.

"She's not that bad, actually." He rested his hand on his chin and began to draw rugby-ball-shaped doodles on a notepad. "I know it's not what we'd planned for tonight."

Ali sat back in her chair. This was interesting.

They had, over the past weeks, made a very distinct point of not having *any* plans. Ever. They'd "just happened" to end up in one or the other's kitchens, or sofas, and just about always beds every single night since "That Night" a few months ago.

"And what exactly *was* it we had planned for tonight?"

"Hanging out with my dad didn't really top the list."

Aidan's face lit up with one of those irascible smiles of his, and despite her best intentions Ali's tummy went all effervescent in a way that had nothing to do with her pregnancy.

"I really need to pack tonight, Aidan."

She tried to look aggrieved at the choice she had to make, but dining out as a family when she knew there was a whole lot more "family" on the cards than anyone else knew was not a chart-topper for her.

"C'mon, Ali. We both know you only have enough things to put in a run bag." His eyes met hers. "I know it's weird, but I'd like you to come. You know me. I'm hardly the king of lively conversation and I promise to be really irritating. It'll make your forget-about-Aidan campaign much easier."

"I don't think anything will make that easier."

Ali wished she could swallow the words back down her throat. She would never, *ever* forget Aidan Tate. Not in a million years.

"Hey... C'mon..." Aidan's fingers crept across the desk toward hers. "It hasn't been all bad, has it?"

"You know it has been the total *opposite* of that, you barmstick."

"Easy on the language, Lockhart. You'll get yourself kicked off the field tomorrow if you don't watch it."

Ali didn't reply. She just gave him a sad smile. She could feel the choke of tears begin in her throat. This was going to be so tough. Harder than anything. Why did he have to carry on being so *nice*? If he could go back to being the irascible, arrogant, know-it-all she'd first met this would be a whole lot easier. But if he really had been that haughty guy she knew she wouldn't have fallen in love with him as deeply as she had.

"Look. I'm not going to take no for an answer. We'll eat early. They're still jet-lagged, and you and I both need an early night." Aidan put his hands up in the air as if he was showing her his final card. His ace. "Besides, you'll need your energy for tomorrow and it's not like you're going to eat well at home." He pulled a face. "I've tasted your cooking."

"What are you saying, exactly? I make delicious bowls of cereal!" Ali was laughing now. He had that way with her. Always teasing away the protective layers and unveiling one of her unabashed smiles when she least expected to give it.

She felt her smile fade and had to look away from those dark eyes of his.

She'd wanted change when she came up here to Tealside, and she had received the superdeluxe treatment.

"So, I'll pick you up around six-thirty?"

Aidan rose from his chair as if it were a done deal. Then he smiled again, the little crinkles by his eyes doing their cute little dimple thing.

It was only dinner. And she was a grown-up. Might as well meet the future grandparents of her child!

"Great. See you then."

# CHAPTER TEN

"AIDAN TELLS US you work with dancers?"

Richard Tate was definitely a man who liked to keep the flow of conversation moving. Not that he had much work on his hands tonight. He and his wife were great fun, and Ali would've been hard pressed to recall a single awkward moment. Even Aidan, whom she'd thought might easily revert into "annoyed son mode," seemed on good form.

"Most of the work I do—*did*—was with dancers. But En Pointe does a lot of work with gymnasts, as well. They have similar injuries. It's mostly women, so working up here has been quite a change."

*Understatement of the universe!*

"Ali's made some great alterations to the team's training."

Aidan jumped in with details of all the changes they'd made since her arrival. In fact all night he'd been on some sort of mission to put all her plus-points on display. It was flattering, sure. But not what she was used to. Particularly after having worked with shut-down, grim-faced Aidan for the past few days.

It felt as though she'd grabbed on to an enormous emotion-laden pendulum and was holding on for dear life. He was acting like a young man showing off his new girlfriend to his parents—not someone who'd brought her along just to keep the chitchat lively. Talk about a sea change.

"I'd like to make sure Ali's work here stays in play." He gave her a wink before taking a bite of his steak.

He liked it medium rare: super-seared on the outside with a dark seam of rare in the center. With chips. And a mountain of salad. Not that she had been getting to know everything he liked over the past three months or anything. *Nothing like that at all.*

"In fact," he continued after a moment, "we might start calling the exercises 'Lockharts.'"

Everyone at the table laughed apart from Ali, who just managed not to choke on her wild mushroom gratin. *Classy.*

Lockharts? *Really?* All that was going to remain of her time here were some ankle-strengthening exercises? Or was all of this just Aidan's way of trying to sugarcoat the truth? He was looking forward to her departure. He liked being in charge. That much had been clear when she'd arrived.

Her hand slipped onto her belly for a protective rub. All she had to do was make it through this dinner and the game tomorrow, and then she would be done. Oh! And tell Aidan he was going to be a father before she hopped on the train. Other than that—she had just about wrapped everything up.

"Are your plans to return to London straight away?" Marianne asked.

"That's the idea," Ali quipped, grabbing her water and fastidiously avoiding eye contact with Aidan.

Her mouth had gone dry about a thousand times already that night and this moment was no different. Until she told Aidan about their baby, and that he was off the hook in the responsibility department, everything was going to be off-kilter. Time to steer the conversation off of her.

"How did you and Richard meet?"

If Ali could've opened her mouth and stuffed her foot directly into it she would have. Aidan stared at her in disbelief until Marianne and Richard broke the silence with near-hysterical giggles.

"I thought Aidan would've told you!"

"Well…" Ali desperately started backpedaling. "He did mention something about—about your profession."

"Don't worry, dear." Marianne reached across the table and patted her arm comfortingly. "I like to look at our introduction as a sort of primer into The Full Richard Tate Package." She gave her new husband a warm smile. "I knew what I was getting into when I agreed to marry this man— and I also knew exactly what sort of woman he didn't want."

"What's ridiculous," Richard jumped in, "is how long it took me to figure it out. They do say women are smarter than men. I can assure you, Ali, that is definitely the case in this scenario. Truth be told, I'm grateful for my past. If I hadn't made so many mistakes, hit rock-bottom, I never would've ended up at this one's doorstep. I'm just annoyed it took me so long to realize Cupid was pointing his big neon arrow right over her cute little head."

He gave Marianne's hand a squeeze and lifted his glass of wine.

"A toast."

Ali raised the glass of wine she'd been fastidiously avoiding all night.

"A toast," Richard repeated, making eye contact with each of them. "To finding 'The One.'"

As Ali raised her glass to the chorus of "Hear! Hear!" her stomach dropped, then catapulted up to her throat.

There had been a ridiculously untethered moment in time when she'd thought Aidan might have been The One—but he had been very clear that family life was not for him. She watched as Richard gave Marianne a moon-eyed gaze, followed by a kiss... If his goal in bringing her here to meet his dad had been to illustrate just how messed up his father was, it wasn't working.

"You're not drinking to the toast?"

Aidan's hand slipped onto her knee under the table. She wished he wouldn't do that. It was all too easy to imagine him touching her elsewhere, and they weren't doing that anymore. She jogged her knee away from his hand.

"I took a sip," she lied. "Just trying to keep my wits about me for the match tomorrow. We're lucky it's a home game, aren't we?"

*Excellent topic-changer, Ali! You're getting good at this.*

"Good point, love." Richard took a final swig of his wine whilst signaling to the waiter that they wanted the check. "We could do with slipping off to bed and letting you both get your rest." He gave a wink to Aidan. "I don't want to shoulder the blame for any poorly set noses tomorrow."

"Dad." Aidan sent his father a dry look. "I think I can handle a broken nose in my sleep, thank you very much."

"I know, son." He gave Aidan a pointed look. "There isn't much you *can't* do once you set your mind to something."

"You really didn't have to walk me to my car. I'm a big girl, you know."

Ali fumbled amidst her handbag debris for her key. Was being discombobulated part of being pregnant? Or was being next to Aidan the reason her well-honed cool demeanor had deteriorated into a jumble of jitters?

"Of course I did. You were incredibly indulgent in accompanying me here. 'Meeting the parents.'" He flicked his fingers in the quotes symbol then put his hands on her shoulders and turned her toward him.

The jangle factor of her nerve endings shot up another notch. He slid his hands along the collar of her coat and tucked it up close round her neck.

*Oh...why do you always have to smell so nice? And be so nice. I don't want to say goodbye.*

The thought lay like lead in her heart. "Right. So, I'll see you at the stadium tomorrow, bright and early?"

"Yeah, of course—the big game!" Aidan let his hands dawdle on her coat collar, his index fingers tracing along the stitched edging of the woolen fabric, thumbs circling in a slow swirl. He'd done it before. That swirl. Her skin remembered it well—her tummy, her breasts... It took all her power not to arch into him, press herself tight against his chest.

But she couldn't do anything to give away what

she was really feeling. Not now that she knew his heart would never belong to her.

They each stared at his fingers—lost, she presumed, in different lines of thought. His mind was on the game... Hers was on—what else?—the new life she carried.

Ali wondered if he could sense the changes she had already noticed. She wasn't showing, but she felt more like a woman than she ever had. She was used to feeling lanky—all legs and arms and a long torso to stick it all together—but here, so close to Aidan, with their child in her belly, she felt about as soft and feminine as they came.

"Ali? It meant a lot to me."

"What? Having dinner? You already said that, silly." She looked up into his eyes. She'd miss exploring their deep brown depths, trying to figure out if they were espresso, mahogany, teak or any other deliciously brown color.

"No, I mean—" He broke off and shot a look in his father's direction. He and his wife were standing beside his car. "You being here. All of it." He ducked his head lower, trying his best to give her a meaningful look.

Ali shrugged herself out of his hold on the

premise of needing to rub her hands together. She didn't need this. Couldn't bear it. Trite good-byes for an affair that had enveloped her body and soul were too painful.

She forced herself to look up at him. He wasn't the man he thought he was. Dispassionate. All business. He was kind. Caring. And *so* off-limits. It tore at her heart that his heart was tethered to the past. If only he could see the future for what it was—an amazing gift.

"Well, all good things must come to an end, right?" If they were going to go with trite she might as well embrace the truisms with a fresh smile.

"You're right." he acquiesced. "What's the point in making rules if you don't stick to them?"

Ali pressed her lips together and gave him what she hoped looked like a nod. She didn't agree. Not now. This was definitely a time when rules were meant to be broken. Meant to be reformed, reshaped. Why not the whole shebang? This was a time when they needed an entirely new rule-book—one that bent and flowed with the wind. One that would allow them to be together. One that allowed them to have a baby.

"Son, we're freezing to death out here. Mind if you toss us the keys?"

"I'm coming, Dad."

Aidan turned to go, then swiftly turned back and bent his head to kiss her on the cheek. It was one of those instants she wished she could have frozen in time. His scent. His touch. His breath slipping along her cheek down to the bit of neck not snuggled in the depths of her woolly scarf. She'd never know those sensations again.

Choking back a sob, Ali nodded again and gave him a wave goodbye. She plunged back into her handbag and came up trumps on the first forage. Car keys. Thank God. She needed to get away. Clear her head. Write the script—the farewell script—and make sure the North Stars won their final match before she set about figuring out what she and her baby would do with the rest of their lives.

Nothing to it. Nothing at all.

"Are you going to tell me why you won't admit to dating that young woman?"

Aidan's father dunked an herbal teabag in and out of his mug as he waited for Aidan to answer.

Since when did Mr. Meat and Potatoes drink *herbal tea*?

"Not sure what you're talking about, Dad."

"Ali. The young woman we just dined with."

His father spoke slowly, as if Aidan had suddenly become hard of hearing.

"We work together. That's all."

"Yes, son, and I'm the Emperor of China." His father laughed, squeezed the teabag on the side of the mug with a spoon and took it out. "You're in love with that woman—it's plain as the hand at the end of my arm."

Aidan all but choked on his own tea. Traditional English tea, with milk in. *He* hadn't changed. Unlike his father, who kept throwing new components of himself out into the universe to be seen by one and all. Wasn't this the man who'd taught him that there was no sure thing in life? That love was as fleeting as the seasons? *It comes and goes—it comes and goes—and you can never rely on it.*

"Sorry, Dad." Aidan gave him a rueful look. "Just colleagues."

His father walked round the kitchen island and

pulled out one of the stools. "Against company rules, is it?"

Aidan's stomach clenched. "Something like that." He nodded, hoping his father would let the subject drop, and took another sip of tea. Against Aidan's rules was more like it, but he didn't need to tell his father that.

"No. I don't buy it, son. What happened? You two have a fight or something?"

Aidan looked at his father in surprise. What was this? An inquisition? "What would make you say something like that?"

"I don't know. There definitely seemed to be something going on between the two of you— but Ali seemed..." He sought the perfect word just as Marianne came into the kitchen, made a beeline for her husband's mug and took a sip. "Sugar, what was that thing you said about Aidan and Ali?"

Aidan's eyebrows just about popped off his forehead. *What*? They'd been *discussing* him and Ali? They'd only been home from supper for five minutes!

Marianne gave him a guilty smile. "Don't worry, love. It's one of the side effects of my trade. I just can't help analyzing every couple I come across."

"We're *not* a couple! How many times do I have to tell you?"

"Well, if you're not you should be," Marianne rejoined. "I have seen thousands of couples come in and out of my offices. Most of them end up divorced. But the ones with a connection like you two have...? Those ones always end up leaving hand in hand."

"Like you and me, eh?" Aidan's father grabbed her round the waist and gave her a cuddle.

"Most of my suitors didn't show up with their wives. Or wait twenty more years to propose, for that matter."

"I wanted to be original!"

"You definitely are that, love. You definitely are that." She gave Richard a peck on the cheek and stole his mug again for another sip.

"We're not a couple," Aidan muttered into his mug, acutely aware that no one was remotely listening to his side of the conversation.

He should just go to bed. Watching these two canoodle was getting him nowhere. The whole reason he'd put a halt to things between Ali and himself was because you couldn't change the past. It was part of you—no matter what.

"Besides, son..." Aidan's father re-engaged him, with Marianne's shoulder safely tucked under his arm. "It's like your mother said the other day—"

"Wait a minute." Aidan could hardly believe his ears. "You still *talk* to Mum?"

"'Course I do, son. We may not have been a love match—and I can assure you we don't talk much—but we've got an eternal bond."

Aidan opened his hands in a *what bond?* gesture.

"*You*, son. We'll always be proud of having done that together. If I hadn't met your mother I wouldn't have you, and there is not a chance in high heaven that I would've gone through my life without knowing the absolute pleasure of fatherhood."

This was a bit of a blindsider.

They'd never really had a traditional father-son relationship. It wasn't as though Aidan had ever felt unloved, he just hadn't felt a part of his father's life, except on an administrative level. Particularly since Mary had died, It was hardly as if his dad had been seeking Father of the Year points.

"That's right, Aidan." Marianne nodded. "In fact your father was quite reluctant about our tying the knot without you being there. He was really hoping you'd join us, but with the season running the way it does he thought you'd be wrapped up in work."

Aidan's face must've been screaming *Seriously?* because both of them burst out laughing.

"It's true, son." His father nodded earnestly. "I was hoping you would be our ring bearer. You would've looked a treat in that 'Little Boy Blue' getup they wear."

Aidan had to join in their laughter. The picture of himself in a little pastel suit with a satin cushion, carrying the rings down the aisle for his father's golden years wedding, was too funny a picture not to laugh at.

"Thanks, Dad. I would've liked to have been there."

"You're always welcome to join us, son. Now that I've found myself a proper wife, who seems intent on keeping me chipper, you are welcome. Anytime."

And from the look on his father's face Aidan could see he meant it. Maybe things really *had* changed for his father. He'd never really invited Aidan along to things before—and he'd always just presumed it was because he didn't want him around.

"Well, son. We're going to pop off to bed. I imagine you'll be up and out of here early. Shall we meet you after the game?"

"That'd be great," Aidan replied with a smile. He meant it, too. "You two have a good night. There will be tickets for you at the gate."

Half an hour later Aidan could still hear them giggling through the walls of the guest bedroom. They really were the picture of a happy couple. Which was a lot more than he could say for Ali and himself. Not that they *were* a couple. They'd been fastidious in that respect—keeping the boundaries clear. Boundaries that had melted away in the bedroom.

Beyond that...? Aidan sank into his sofa, barely seeing the twinkling lights of the city beyond.

He and Ali worked well together. Played well together. They did just about *everything* well together. But was that because they'd made their time limit? Set the boundaries? Was that the only way he functioned? By being able to shut and lock the door on his feelings? It was the way he'd always worked after he'd lost his girlfriend, and it had worked perfectly well. Until now.

Aidan shook his head and pushed up from the sofa. He'd better get some sleep before the match. The last day he'd work with Ali. The last time they would be together. He would never hold her in his arms again.

He hastened to remind himself that it was all for one very pragmatic and practiced reason: he didn't do affairs of the heart. There would be no honoring of what he'd had—or could have had—with Mary if he did. They would have been married now—maybe even had children...

The thought sent a sour taste down his throat. He'd always wanted a family. A big one to make up for his pretty lonely excuse of a childhood. He just had to face facts now. Once Ali was gone he could get back to structure, routine, to his well-practiced comfort zone.

He pulled the duvet up around his head as if it would help block out the truth. This time it had been different. He'd stepped outside the outline of their agreement. This time he'd fallen in love.

Ali felt as though she was having a flashback to the first day she'd met Aidan. Well...not *that* day. Their first day at work. She was kneeling on the ground next to Rory and could see Aidan's size eleven shoes in her eyeline. Only this time he was letting her get on with things. At least they'd made progress in the professional respect department.

"How's it feeling, Rory?"

"Just a turf burn, Doc. It's that new artificial turf. Doesn't suit my baby-soft skin." He tried to wink away her concerns.

"Rory! You were writhing around clutching your shoulder."

"It's not my shoulder. Honest. Just giving the crowd a bit of bonus drama." He popped up from the field with a grin, despite the expanse of raw skin on his arm. "C'mon!" he pleaded. "We've got to get this show on the road! We're three up!"

Ali turned to consult Aidan—who, she could now see, was already jogging back to the benches. *Terrific.* So much for a conference with her colleague. She guessed it was going to be a day of his and hers injuries.

He had hardly said *boo* to her all day. "Exasperating" didn't begin to explain how frustrating the situation was. Where had the "Chatty Kathy" from the night before gone? They were back to the days of Dr. Jekyll and Aidan Hyde. Hide 'n' seek was more like it. The man had been avoiding her from the moment they'd arrived at the stadium.

Or maybe she was just being super-sensitive. They were all hopped up today. The boys were definitely running on high-caliber adrenaline.

The team as a whole had only clocked up a couple of minor injuries, and if they carried on as they had been they'd charge through the rest of the game like bulls. They were super-charged. Everyone was. This was the biggest match of the year, and it felt as if the whole of England had jammed itself into the stands. The roar of the crowd was deafening.

If only it could stifle all the thoughts lurching round her head like out-of-control billiard balls— clanking against each other before careening off in an entirely different direction.

Some focus might be in order.

After a quick examination to make sure his collarbone was still in one piece Ali nodded a reluctant assent. Play could recommence. She jogged off the pitch and headed toward a different bench than the one Aidan had chosen. The number of times she'd almost blurted out her news in the past hour alone was running into double digits.

She glanced up at the game clock. Thirty-seven more minutes. That was it. Thirty-seven minutes and the game would be over, the trophy would—Lord willing—be in the hands of the North Stars, and she could let Aidan know she was pregnant then jump on the train and go back to her old life.

It was what she had decided in the witching hours of the previous night. She had enjoyed setting up En Pointe, and now that she had a baby on the way maybe being around people she knew wouldn't be such a bad thing. Not that that wasn't the case here.

She took a mental panoramic shot of the stadium in its full glory. Leaving the team behind—the work she'd begun with them, her apartment, the bicycle rides, all of it—was going to be much harder than she'd thought. And as for leaving Aidan...

Pure, unadulterated denial was the only way she was going to get through that goodbye.

Would she prefer to stay with him and watch their baby grow up together? There wasn't a *yes* big enough to encapsulate how much she wanted that to be the case. But there was no getting away from the fact that it was absolutely *not* what Aidan wanted. And she couldn't blame him. He hadn't exactly been handed the smoothest ride in life. No doubt the pain of moving forward— moving on and away from what had never been... Well... He'd made it clear that was never going to happen.

She pressed her hands together between her knees and forced herself to focus on the game. The two sides were going into formation for a new play. What had originally been a massive huddle of muscles and numbered shirts now pinged into individual components for her. She saw repaired ligaments, strengthened ankle joints, improved flexibility, increased speed, heightened stamina. These were some of the fittest people on earth and she had played a role in keeping them that way. Making them more than what they'd thought they could be. It was truly satisfying work.

The huddle of men broke apart as play recommenced, with players running long to catch the rugby ball spinning toward them in a meters-high arc. Mack, unsurprisingly, was at the center of the action, arms reaching up high, cleats giving him the traction to push harder, further than the other players. But as he leapt into the air his arms suddenly snapped to his chest, his feet giving way to the bend of his knees as he crumpled to the ground.

It took the rest of the players a moment to realize anything had happened, but Ali had already taken off from her bench at full speed, calling for a defibrillator to be brought immediately. Everything she knew about him reeled through her mind. The consistently low heart-rate, the intense training, his young age, the occasional bouts of dizziness during training he had always put down to getting overheated.

*Hypertrophic cardiomyopathy.*

She should have seen it earlier. All the signs would've come together if they had scanned all of the players like the Italians were required to.

*Mack was having a heart attack.* Sudden cardiac death in young athletes had been hitting the headlines too often lately, and it looked like this match would now hit the front page for all the wrong reasons.

As each microsecond passed his life would be in increasing danger. Her lungs tightened as she ran faster. Aidan passed her with an AED kit before she'd even become aware of him. He had obviously put the pieces of the puzzle together, as well. The crowd went collectively silent as Ali reached the group of players around Mack.

One of the opposing team players was already doing compressions on Mack's chest.

"Did you check the airway?" Aidan knelt down opposite the player.

"Yes, Doc. No heartbeat."

The player continued his compressions until Aidan indicated that they should switch roles. "Ali! Grab the AED."

She took the player's place, checking the switches on the automated external defibrillator. They glowed green. Aidan must've flicked it on while running. These portable devices were a godsend in this sort of scenario. The only truly effective way to shock the heart back into action.

If Mack's heart was strong enough...

Without seeing a scan it was impossible to say, but Ali would have bet any amount of money it would reveal a thickened wall of heart muscle around the septum, where the left and right sides of the heart were separated. When the muscle between the lower heart chambers thickened blood flow could be blocked—particularly when the body was undergoing intense physical strain.

"Pulse?" Aidan looked to her for an answer.

Ali placed her fingers on both Mack's wrist and his carotid artery. *Nothing.* She shook her head.

"Are you charged?"

"Yes."

Ali rucked up Mack's shirt, stopping only for Aidan to finish a series of compressions. He lifted his hands so she could place the electrode pads on his bare chest. She gave each cable a quick tug to ensure they were firmly in place.

"Clear!"

Aidan raised his hands. She pressed the shock button and watched as the voltage bucked through Mack's chest. Aidan began chest compressions again. Thirty chest compressions and then two breaths of air. It would be up to two minutes before the AED could read Mack's obs and let them know if it had worked—if they'd tricked his body into working again.

She held her breath along with the rest of the crowd, her eyes trained on Aidan's woven fingers as he pressed the ball of his hand into Mack's chest again and again.

She tried to picture everything happening inside of the young player's body. With his heart in a state of ventricular fibrillation nerve impulses would still be shooting from the brain, but so irregularly the heart would not be receiving a strong enough message to continue expelling blood into the circulatory system.

The AED should have shocked his heart into a regular heartbeat...

"Again."

She didn't need to be asked twice. It hadn't worked. She'd already prepped the charging pads with gel.

"Clear!"

Aidan began compressions again. At least two minutes had passed. Two incredibly precious minutes. The microscopic child inside her would have found it impossible to battle those odds. Mack was a fit twenty-two-year-old man. She prayed he had better chances.

After four to six minutes the brain would begin to suffer from oxygen deprivation and cells would begin to die. Each second ticking away as Aidan's hands systematically pulsed out an artificial heartbeat were buying time for the shock they'd just sent through Mack's body to stop the heart's spasm. If it worked this time his nerve impulses would resume their normal pattern and his heart would resume its normal pacing. If it was strong enough.

"Twenty-nine. Thirty."

They both leaned back on their heels and looked at the AED for a reading.

It was slight. But it was there.

Relief washed through Ali. It was near impossible to hold back the tears. Mack had made it. He wasn't out of the woods, but he was with them. She looked up, surprised to realize that an ambulance had arrived on the pitch and the players had formed an orderly row, heads all bowed as each man made a silent prayer for his fellow player.

"Load him up!" Aidan called to the medics. "You'll be all right?"

Aidan rubbed a hand along her arm as he indicated that he would be going along with the paramedics to the hospital. It was impossible to tell if his eyes were asking her something more—something deeper.

She *would* be all right. One day.

As Ali watched the ambulance doors closing Aidan out of her sight, she felt all of her senses come back into play, as if she'd flicked them off one by one in order to focus on Mack. Sight, sound, touch—everything returned to her with an added appreciation that she was there at all. She was aware of the scent of the grass, the somber applause from the crowd as the ambulance left the arena, the bright, bright blue sky above them on the crisp March day. The gratitude she felt for the gift of life growing within her.

Ali's hands slipped to her belly as she strode off the playing field. It was growing within her. Life. *Precious, precious life.* And she would do everything in her power to make sure her baby had the best shot at happiness she could offer.

\* \* \*

The ride to the hospital had been tense, to say the least. Mack's heart had failed again. And one more time as they'd entered the A&E courtyard. Aidan had ridden atop the gurney, pressing an endless flow of syncopated pulses into Mack's body, willing his young heart to hold on.

A half hour later the player was still in Critical Care, but had been stabilized for the time being. Aidan stood outside his room, barely hearing the beeps and whirrs of all the equipment the young man was connected to. Hypertrophic cardiomyopathy. It would change Mack's life forever.

He should stick around to tell him the news. It wasn't the sort of thing he should hear from a stranger. His family—parents and two sisters, who had been watching the game—had been told. They were surrounding him now, his mother holding on to her son's hand as if it would give him the extra strength he needed. Perhaps it would. He wouldn't know about that sort of thing. His mother hadn't stuck around long enough to see him through much of anything.

Aidan turned away from the room and shrugged off the thought. He'd passed being bitter about

that part of his life long ago. It was just one of the
compartments he'd shut and closed before he'd
moved on to the next compartment and the next.

His phone bleeped as a message appeared on
the screen. It was Coach Stone.

We won. Tell the boy.

He looked back at Mack's room with a smile.
At least he would have some good news when
he woke up.

# CHAPTER ELEVEN

ALI KNEW HIDING out in the ICU wasn't the most secret of locations, but her fingers were crossed that Aidan wanted to enjoy the celebrations with the team. She'd seen neither hide nor hair of him when she'd arrived in the department, and had just assumed he'd stayed with the team after he'd returned to update them about Mack.

Visiting hours were over, so Mack's family had had to leave. Ali had pushed her train journey to London back a few hours so she could sit with him a bit. If he woke up over the course of the evening it'd be nice for him to have someone there he knew.

She pulled a chair over from the corner of the room and parked it next to Mack, who was sleeping like a baby. A big, muscly baby, who had scared the living daylights out of everyone on and off the pitch today. He'd have some big decisions to make about his future. He was an amazing player, and rugby was his very raison d'être. But was it worth it if the sport could take his life? Maybe he would take a page out of Jonesey's book and go back to uni.

Ali looked upward to the invisible heavens, grateful that her decisions weren't life or death. She propped an elbow on the side of Mack's bed and cupped her chin in her hand. Her decisions were very much about life. Her life. Her baby's. Aidan's...

"Oh, Mack..." she whispered. "How am I going to tell him?"

"Tell him what?"

Ali froze at the sound of Aidan's voice. She barely trusted herself to turn around, let alone start speaking. There was a pretty big list she could spool out. She could tell him she was carrying his child—their child. Tell him she wanted to keep it more than anything in the world, which had completely taken her by surprise.

Falling pregnant had already made her feel more alive than she could possibly have imagined. More accurately, falling pregnant by the man she was absolutely bonkers, head-over-heels in love with had brought out a side of her she'd never known existed. A life-charged, high-beamed wonder that just being alive could be so good—and so heartbreakingly difficult.

She could tell him all those things. But she wanted to make it easier for him. Make the transition back into his old life fluid. Simple. She wanted him to be happy.

"Is it Mack? Any updates?"

Ali swiped at the tears threatening to spill onto her cheeks. "Yes. No. I mean, he's stable. Not totally out of the woods yet—but he'll make it. Indications are he has a strong enough heart to beat this."

*If only hers was as strong.*

"Excellent work out there on the field today."

The compliment felt like one she might get from one of the players. One usually accompanied by a punch on the arm or a playful elbow-jab. Was that ultimately how he saw her? As one of the lads? A ladette with benefits?

She let her head fall back into her hands as her mouth formed into a silent scream.

*Nooooooooooooooooooooo!*

She'd told herself again and again that that was the reality, but there had been a part of her that had believed otherwise. Had hoped he might love her.

How could she have let herself be so foolish? She cracked an eye open, sizing up Aidan through her fingers. He was still there. He was looking deeply uncomfortable, but he was still there. Each gorgeous little centimeter of him, his brow rising in—bewilderment? Concern?

A deep-seated sense of resolve began to steady her, to clear her thoughts, so that only a single truth remained. She was having a baby and would do anything in the world to protect it. Aidan had a right to know. Then she and her baby could get on with their lives.

"Is there somewhere we can talk?"

Aidan put down the paper cups of tea on the table and closed the door to the conference room they'd slipped into. Ali had been worryingly silent as they'd first gone to the cafeteria, then wandered through the hospital trying to find a quiet corner.

What on earth could she need to tell him behind closed doors?

As the door clicked into place, so too did the bits of information whirling around his head.

Each little piece dropped into perfect place. The nausea. The dizziness. Those looks weighted with so much more than the feelings of a woman building up to a bittersweet farewell.

"You're pregnant."

Everything went into a strange slow motion. A feeling akin to seeing the towering waves arch and curve toward him all those years ago. He could hear the roar of the ocean in his ears as he watched Ali nod a confirmation, her teeth pressing into her lower lip, her eyes trained on him.

"How far along?"

"About eight weeks or more. I haven't had a scan yet."

He skimmed a mental calendar. On or around Valentine's Day. The first day he'd laid eyes on Miss Cosmopolitan and wanted, more than anything, to make her his.

"And you want to...?"

The words coming out of his mouth bore no relation to the thoughts pitching between his heart and his mind. *A child?* A baby to care for and raise and assure that the world was a safe, secure place to live in?

"I am going to keep it."

Ali's eyes sparked with a determination he'd not seen in her before—and that was saying something.

She raised a hand before he could interject. "Don't worry. I'm not expecting anything."

"Are you sure?"

The question came out before he could stem it. It wasn't that he wanted there *not* to be a baby—extraordinarily, that wasn't it at all. But this was a life-changing piece of information to take in. And she had already decided his role for him—or rather the absence of a role.

How well she knew him. She saw through his shoddy veneer of calm and bored straight to the heart of the matter. She already knew he wasn't someone who could give Ali or the baby—*his child*—the stability and commitment they deserved. Sure, he did steady as they came within the confines of work—but outside the stadium... They had agreed on a one-time, one-place deal—and she was holding up her end of the bargain.

The white noise in his head grew even louder. Was it actually possible to hear the cogs whirling between one's ears? He rubbed at his temples, the roar making it impossible to train his focus on exactly what he wanted—needed—to do.

Ali was watching him with cool reserve. She was unreadable. As the words had come out of his mouth he'd known they were off-center, but the future Ali had placed before him was one he had never let himself consider and she knew it. He'd been more than clear on that matter. Aidan Tate didn't do long-term.

He looked into her eyes, searching for an answer—the right answer. Was she telling him what she really wanted? To be a single mother? From what he knew of Ali, she felt as let down by love as he did. Striking out on her own would be the safest way to go.

She arched an eyebrow as if daring him to question her decision. She was telling him what she wanted loud and clear. *Get out of my life.*

"I'm happy to contribute."

*Pathetic! C'mon, man. You're better than this!*

"Don't worry. I'm fine in that department."

"Of course. But you will let me know if—?"

She gave him a sad smile with a shake of her head and pushed up from the table. "I will."

He couldn't help letting his eyes linger on her

waistline as she rose. His fingertips twitched at the thought of the smooth expanse of skin beneath the loose swing of her jumper. His hands knew every contour of her body. The dip from her rib cage along her belly—a belly that would soon grow round and pronounced. A belly he could rest his hand on and wait, eyes locked with hers, for a hiccough or a kick.

"Ali—" He rose with her and reached out.

If he could just hold her in his arms for a minute—rest his cheek on that silky black hair of hers and have a chance to digest everything— maybe he could fix this.

That her gut reaction was to pull back with a flinch told him all he needed to know. She was ready to move on and he needed to respect that. Aidan was no longer part of her life. What happened to her was now her business and hers only.

Silence was the best thing he could muster as she picked up her bag and spun her woolen scarf around her neck. If he told her he loved her he would only make things worse, more painful. As she did up the buttons of her coat it was all he could do to stop himself from asking her to stay, to see what would happen if they gave "being real" a chance. Being human—open to the aches and pains and joys of loving someone.

"Goodbye, Aidan."

She laid her hand on his shoulder for just a moment. And then she was gone.

Where are you????? Ali sent the message and took another scan of the bar. Trust Cole to ask a pregnant woman to meet him at a *bar*. He was going to be the most inappropriate godfather going, but he was her best friend and—like it or not—he was all she had right now when it came to family.

As soon as the tease of tears began to sting at the back of her throat she took another gulp of water. *Swallow it down. It's just the hormones. Everything's good. Exactly as you want it.*

No Aidan. No broken heart.

She took another gulp of water. One day she'd believe her new mantra. *Really.* She would. It had already been over a week since she'd left and she was virtually swinging from the rafters with all the freedom she was feeling. Seriously. She *was*.

She caught a glimpse of herself in the bar mirror. Frowning. Big-time.

Okay. Maybe she'd have to work on the footloose and fancy-free thing a bit—but she'd get there.

"For the lady."

Ali looked up at the bartender in surprise. He was placing a Cosmopolitan onto a bar mat in front of her. Er...this was going to be awkward.

"The gentleman wanted me to say it's alcohol-free." The bartender gave her a look, as if to say he knew it was weird, too, but whatever, he was just doing his job.

Ali's heart lurched, before taking off at an accelerated rate. She hardly trusted herself to turn around. It would have been a bit of a no-brainer for Aidan to find her at the clinic if he'd wanted to, but over a week had gone by and she hadn't heard a peep.

She stared at the icy rim of the cocktail glass as if it would turn into an oracle and give her some answers. Only one man knew that was her drink. A mug of tea was slid onto the bar alongside her cocktail. She arched an eyebrow at it. Not quite what she had been expecting.

"I thought I'd lay off the wine to keep you company."

Aidan's voice swept along Ali's spine, unleashing an all-over spray of body shivers. For goodness' sake! A few goosebumps along her arms was not good enough? *Hormones, definitely.* Had to be hormones. Not the fact that the love of her life had just appeared beside her.

"Mind if I sit down?"

Ali's hand automatically moved to her belly as she turned to face him. It was almost impossible to believe how happy she felt at the sight of him. Suppressing the smile she knew she wanted to give him was a mammoth task, but she did it. Aidan didn't have a right to be here. Not while she was patching up her heart.

"I'd rather you didn't."

"Even if I am prepared to announce to everyone in this bar—or the whole of London, for that matter—the fact that I've been a complete and utter idiot?"

Ali felt her lips twitch, teasing at her composure. She leaned back and gave him an appraising look. "Depends upon just how big an idiot you think you've been."

"Oh, I can assure you…" Aidan drummed his fingers along the bar-top as if his body was humming with as much excess energy as hers was. "I have been a *colossal* idiot. Epic-style. So much so I've been nominated Chief Idiot of Idiotsville and I expect to win."

A full smile lit up her face. She couldn't help it. Aidan had a way of bringing out Fun Ali with just one of those knowing winks of his. She really was going to have to toughen up if keeping this man out of her life was her goal. It *was* her goal. Wasn't it?

"I suppose my mate at En Pointe is behind all of this?" She pushed the stool next to hers out from under the bar so that he could join her.

"I didn't really think I stood much chance if I tried to get in touch with you."

"Mmm... Well..." She felt her smile fade away. "I think you were more than clear about where you stood when we last spoke."

"That's just it, Ali. I wasn't clear at all." Aidan reached out for her hand.

She balled it up like a fist inside his fingers. *No! You don't get access to me. Not now. Not now that I have a baby to protect.*

Aidan kept his hand on hers, his thumb rubbing along the surface of her fist. Back and forth.

Back and forth. Soothing her. Like he would a child. She couldn't do this. Ali pulled her hand away and crossed her arms protectively across her chest.

"Ali," Aidan persisted. "I was wrong. About everything."

"When you say everything—what exactly are you talking about? 'Everything' covers a pretty big—"

"I mean about the baby, about you, about me and how we all fit in together."

Ali sucked her lower lip into her mouth, pushing it back and forth along the edge of her teeth as if it would add clarity to what he was saying.

"And what conclusion did you reach?"

"That I needed to grow up, move on."

"What do you mean? Move on from—?"

"From the island and what happened there."

"So…have you found a way to do that?"

"I think I have. First—and it took my dad, of all people, to come up with this one—I would like to set up a scholarship fund, so more people there can train in medicine. I mean, it won't be huge—but it would be a help."

Ali nodded along. That sounded good. Really good. Healing...

"And secondly..."

He paused and cleared his throat—first once, then a second time—then twisted a swizzle stick into a knot.

"Are you keeping that one a secret or have you just come down here to torture me?" Ali teased, her heart careening round her rib cage.

He looked up at her and pulled her hands into his, eyes bright with emotion.

"I'm trying, Alexis Lockhart—defender of the people—in a really bad, terribly awkward way, to ask you to marry me."

Ali's eyes popped wide open. She felt the word *yes* form in her mouth but couldn't get her lips and tongue to join in on the action. She loved Aidan, heart and soul. Loved him as she had never loved another—particularly now that she had this little teensy, tiny baby of his tucked up safe and sound in her belly. But he'd never expressed any desire for a wife, a family...

"Don't answer yet." Aidan put a finger to her lips. "None of this is how I wanted it to be."

"I thought you never wanted *any* of this to be?" Ali indicated the two of them and then her belly.

"A few short months ago you would've been absolutely right."

"And then what happened?"

"You."

"Aidan—don't." Ali fixed him with her steeliest gaze. She had to. There weren't many more trips through the emotional wringer she could survive. "We had a one-night stand at an airport."

"Alexis Lockhart, what we had was most certainly more than a one-night stand. I began to fall in love with you that night, and fate gave me a chance to put things right."

"How? By making it clear that the last thing you wanted was a relationship?"

"Making me face the truth is more like it. I messed things up. I know I did. It's just—I thought you deserved more. So much more than I believed I was capable of giving. But the day you left it became ridiculously clear I was making the hugest mistake of my life. Even my dad could see things more clearly than I could. But now I can. I wouldn't be honoring what was good about my past by keeping my heart clamped shut for the rest of my life. And you—my sweet, amazing, irascible, sexy tigress of a wonder woman—you made my heart come to life again, and I want nothing more than to create a family with you."

He took her hand in his and pressed his lips to it.

"Ali, you are the woman I love—heart and soul. I would be the happiest man alive if you agreed to marry me."

It was all Ali could do to stop herself from nodding like a lunatic. If she hadn't known better she would've sworn her heart was soaring round inside her rib cage—held aloft by little tweeting birds. She loved Aidan with all of her heart, but she wasn't just making a decision for one now. She had to be sure he meant what he said.

"You know there are going to be changes in your life if I say yes? Lots of them?"

"The day I met you my life changed—for the better. You've taught me what my dad has known all along—that love is worth taking a risk for. Worth changing for."

"Well..." Ali toyed with a cocktail swizzler. "When you put it that way..."

"Ali." Aidan placed his hands on either side of her face. "I love you. Please say you'll marry me."

"Do we have to tell our baby about the airport?"

Aidan's laugh lines crinkled as his lips formed a broad smile. "Is this a yes?"

"Only if you promise to keep that little nugget of information our very own secret." Ali rested her forehead on his, closing her eyes as she took a deep breath of him. It was as if breathing him in made her whole again.

"I promise." Aidan gave her a soft peck on the lips. "And I promise never to tell the next baby we have, or the next one." He kissed and teased at her lips as he continued, "Or the next one..."

"How many babies are we going to have?" Ali laughed, slipping her arms over his shoulders.

"Oh, I was thinking a dozen or so." He pulled back, eyes twinkling.

"Oh, *reeeeally?* That was what you were thinking?" She tipped her head to the side as Aidan traced a finger along her jawline.

"I thought we could have our own little rugby squad."

Ali was giggling like a lunatic now. "Is that what you thought?"

"Oh, I could think of quite a few things for us to do over the years. But I know what we could do right now..." He pulled out the key to a hotel room and flashed it between his fingers like a magician.

"What do you say to a one-million-night stand?"

"One million?"

Ali gave him a kiss, then pulled back to study his face. That perfectly gorgeous face she would love until the end of time.

"I don't think that will be nearly long enough, but I'm happy to give it a go."

\* \* \* \* \*

# MILLS & BOON®
## Large Print Medical

## August

| | |
|---|---|
| His Shock Valentine's Proposal | Amy Ruttan |
| Craving Her Ex-Army Doc | Amy Ruttan |
| The Man She Could Never Forget | Meredith Webber |
| The Nurse Who Stole His Heart | Alison Roberts |
| Her Holiday Miracle | Joanna Neil |
| Discovering Dr Riley | Annie Claydon |

## September

| | |
|---|---|
| The Socialite's Secret | Carol Marinelli |
| London's Most Eligible Doctor | Annie O'Neil |
| Saving Maddie's Baby | Marion Lennox |
| A Sheikh to Capture Her Heart | Meredith Webber |
| Breaking All Their Rules | Sue MacKay |
| One Life-Changing Night | Louisa Heaton |

## October

| | |
|---|---|
| Seduced by the Heart Surgeon | Carol Marinelli |
| Falling for the Single Dad | Emily Forbes |
| The Fling That Changed Everything | Alison Roberts |
| A Child to Open Their Hearts | Marion Lennox |
| The Greek Doctor's Secret Son | Jennifer Taylor |
| Caught in a Storm of Passion | Lucy Ryder |

# MILLS & BOON®
## Large Print Medical

## November

| | |
|---|---|
| **Tempted by Hollywood's Top Doc** | Louisa George |
| **Perfect Rivals...** | Amy Ruttan |
| **English Rose in the Outback** | Lucy Clark |
| **A Family for Chloe** | Lucy Clark |
| **The Doctor's Baby Secret** | Scarlet Wilson |
| **Married for the Boss's Baby** | Susan Carlisle |

## December

| | |
|---|---|
| **The Prince and the Midwife** | Robin Gianna |
| **His Pregnant Sleeping Beauty** | Lynne Marshall |
| **One Night, Twin Consequences** | Annie O'Neil |
| **Twin Surprise for the Single Doc** | Susanne Hampton |
| **The Doctor's Forbidden Fling** | Karin Baine |
| **The Army Doc's Secret Wife** | Charlotte Hawkes |

## January

| | |
|---|---|
| **Taming Hollywood's Ultimate Playboy** | Amalie Berlin |
| **Winning Back His Doctor Bride** | Tina Beckett |
| **White Wedding for a Southern Belle** | Susan Carlisle |
| **Wedding Date with the Army Doc** | Lynne Marshall |
| **Capturing the Single Dad's Heart** | Kate Hardy |
| **Doctor, Mummy...Wife?** | Dianne Drake |